TRUE NORTH

A NATION STANDS

KEITH LANDRY

TRUE NORTH: A NATION STANDS

A bold, gripping, and unnervingly real vision of the near future—True North: A Nation Stands will leave you breathless.

Readers are already calling it "blown away," "riveting," and "a call to action."

"I had a sneak peek, and it was a page-turner—I couldn't put it down. We live in turbulent, uncertain times, hoping for the best but bracing for the worst. But what if the worst is closer than we think? Our bad guys are someone else's good guys. This book offers profound insights into the world we're heading toward."

A must-read for Canadians and Americans alike, True North: A Nation Stands delivers a pulse-pounding exploration of what happens when economic collapse pushes Canada to the brink—and the United States sees an opportunity too good to pass up.

How far would a nation go to survive? And who gets to decide its fate?

Turn the page and find out.

Copyright © 2025 by Keith Landry

All rights reserved.

No part of this book may be reproduced in any form or by any electronic or mechanical means, including information storage and retrieval systems, without written permission from the author, except for the use of brief quotations in a book review.

CONTENTS

Introduction	vii
Prologue	1

PART I
LINES ARE DRAWN

1. The Announcement	11
2. Friday Beers at Hustlers	23
3. Premiers' Zoom Meeting	31
4. True North	39
5. American Power	51
6. Calm Before the Storm	59

PART II
MEASURES TAKE EFFECT

7. Ontario's Economy is Suffering	71
8. The Made-Up Leader	81
9. Pain Begins to Reveal Itself	93
10. One of the Moles	101
11. The Belligerent	109
12. Blue Rodeo Concert	119
13. The Tariff Tragedy	131
14. Dialogue	141
15. The Red River Border Skirmish	153
16. Unusual Ally	163
17. A Champion Speaks	175
18. The Letter Campaign	185
19. Canadian Politics	195
20. The FBI's Shift – Canada as an "Enemy"	203
21. The Triumvirate Crumbles	207
22. Detained in Chicago	221

23. Power Dwindling 227
24. Farewell, Lenny 235

Post Note 241
Acknowledgments 249
About the Author 251
Also by Keith Landry 255

INTRODUCTION
A NATION UNDER THREAT

This book was written in haste—not out of carelessness, but out of necessity. When the sovereignty of Canada is under siege, there is no time to waste.

This is a story about resistance—about what governments can do and, more importantly, about what ordinary Canadians must do when their nation faces economic warfare and political aggression from its closest ally turned adversary. It is told in a storytelling fashion because the reality of such a threat is best understood not in cold facts and policy briefs, but through the lives of those who must fight it.

The characters you will meet in these pages are fictional. The events and circumstances are imagined. But the danger they face? The existential threat of annexation, the erosion of democracy, and the manipulation of economies for political control—that is very real.

We do not need to look far to see the warning signs.

- The CIA has operated illegally in Canada before—a fact exposed by Edward Snowden.
- Prime Minister Justin Trudeau has warned Canada's business leaders that the threat of American annexation is not fantasy—it is a possibility.
- The erosion of constitutional safeguards in the United States and the rise of oligarchic control and right-wing autocracy threaten not only Americans but also their closest neighbours.

For this story, Artificial Intelligence was used to swiftly analyze economic data, illustrating the devastating consequences of an economic war on both sides of the border. The numbers are real. The impacts are real. And the lesson is clear:

Canada must be prepared to fight.

At its heart, this book is a call to vigilance—not just for Canadians, but for our American friends. Because if democracy falters in the U.S., it will shake the foundations of freedom everywhere.

The question is whether Americans will rise against creeping autocracy before it is too late.

This is a fictional scenario, but the stakes could not be more real.

I hope you enjoy the story. More importantly, I hope it makes you think.

PROLOGUE

The Greenland Gambit

Greenland – Capital City of Nuuk

The darkness over Nuuk was undisturbed. A quiet, frozen capital, untouched by war. The people of Greenland had always been proud of their vast, unspoiled land, their peaceful way of life.

But tonight, America had come.

The first helicopters arrived just before dawn.

MH-60 Black Hawks, their rotors slicing through the frigid air, swept in low over the snow-covered city, the howl of their engines shattering the silence. Shadows moved in the dim Arctic twilight—fast, disciplined, deadly.

From the open doors, U.S. Navy SEAL teams roped down onto the roof of Greenland's parliamentary complex. The government was asleep, oblivious to what was unfolding above them.

On the docks, three Greenlandic fishers stood huddled against the cold, their hands wrapped around tin mugs of coffee. The sea was calm, the wind sharp. A normal morning—until they saw them.

Black-clad soldiers, their weapons held tight, poured from small assault boats, storming the shoreline in a coordinated assault. The fishermen stood frozen.

One of them, an older man named Svend, instinctively reached for the radio clipped to his vest. He never had the chance to use it.

A warning shot split the air. The crack of suppressed gunfire echoed off the buildings.

The second shot wasn't a warning.

Two of the men collapsed, writhing in the snow, blood staining the pristine white. The third dropped to his knees, hands raised, surrendering to an enemy he had never expected to see.

On the radio inside Greenland's only police station, a voice crackled to life.

"Nuuk is under attack."

By the time the message reached Copenhagen, the American flag had already been raised.

The invasion had taken one hour.

Washington D.C. – The Oval Office

President Jefferson Harland sat behind the Resolute Desk, his expression one of calculated resolve. The cameras were rolling. The country—hell, the world—was watching.

"My fellow Americans," he began, his voice smooth, unwavering. "Early this morning, American forces took decisive action in Greenland."

He let the words hang for a moment. He wanted them to land. He wanted people to feel the weight of what had just happened.

"For too long, foreign influences have sought to destabilize this critical region," he continued. "Greenland, rich in resources, vital to our national security, has been targeted by adversaries who seek to exploit its strategic location. We could not, and would not, allow that to happen."

He paused, watching the teleprompter. He knew the truth, of course—there had been no 'adversaries,' no threats, no aggression. But none of that mattered.

"We were provoked," he said solemnly. "And America does not tolerate provocation."

As his words carried across the airwaves, the lower third of the screen flashed:

BREAKING: PRESIDENT HARLAND ANNOUNCES, 'DEFENSIVE ACTION' IN GREENLAND.

The American people would believe what they were told. They always did.

The Pentagon – War Room

General Randall "Randy" Lutz was in his element.

The chairperson of the Joint Chiefs of Staff sat at the head of the operations table, reviewing footage of the Greenland assault. The speed. The precision. The efficiency.

He leaned back, arms crossed over his massive chest, a satisfied grin tugging at his lips.

"Flawless," he muttered.

The SEALs had executed the mission perfectly. The enemy hadn't stood a chance—hell if you could even call them an enemy. Fishermen and police officers weren't exactly an opposing force.

Lutz had been hoping for more. More resistance. More action. More combat.

When Harland had signed off on the Greenland operation, Lutz had felt a long-dormant hunger stir inside him.

The kind of hunger that could only be fed on the battlefield.

But there had been no battle. Only a swift, surgical strike.

He exhaled sharply. It was still a win.

A young intelligence officer hesitated beside him. "Sir, we're getting early responses from NATO. Denmark's government is calling this an act of war."

Lutz snorted. "What the hell are they gonna do? Throw snowballs at us?"

A chuckle rippled around the room.

Harland had made the call, and Lutz had been thrilled to execute it. Greenland was a prize—a strategic gem. Rare earth minerals. Oil. A location that controlled the Arctic. And best of all, it had been taken without real opposition.

War, without the mess.

He only wished it had been more of a fight.

Copenhagen – Prime Minister's Office

The Danish Prime Minister was trembling with fury.

Standing at the podium, he clutched the edges, his knuckles white. Cameras flashed. The world was watching.

"I want to make something absolutely clear," he said, voice sharp with anger. "Greenland is Danish territory. This act—

this blatant violation of international law—is nothing short of an invasion."

He exhaled, the rage boiling inside him.

"Let me repeat what I told President Harland when he offered to buy Greenland last year." His gaze hardened. "I told him to go fuck himself."

Gasps from the press corps.

"I say the same thing today."

The White House – Crisis Meeting

Harland leaned back in his chair, listening as Margaret Kellerman read the latest diplomatic cables.

"NATO is in emergency session," she said. "The EU is demanding an immediate withdrawal. The UN Secretary-General is calling for sanctions. Russia is saying nothing."

Harland smirked. "Because Russia loves this."

Kellerman hesitated. "Mr. President, this is an escalation—"

"Margaret," Harland interrupted, eyes glinting with amusement. "This is a victory."

Across the room, Lutz gave a firm nod. "Damn right it is."

The general was pleased. He had wanted action, and he had gotten it. He had put boots on the ground, had executed a flawless military operation, and America had won.

Harland turned to Kellerman. "And what's the mood in the country?"

She checked her tablet. "Your base is ecstatic. The opposition is calling it reckless."

Harland smirked. "So, nothing new."

Lutz leaned forward. "Sir, with respect, if NATO wants a fight, we should give it to them. We have control. We have momentum. Let's not back down now."

Harland eyed him carefully. Lutz was a warrior. The kind of man who didn't hesitate.

Harland preferred wars of economy, of media, of control. But Lutz? Lutz wanted something more tangible.

"We'll see how they respond," Harland said finally. "But if they push us, General, I'll give you what you want."

Lutz grinned.

He hoped they pushed.

The World Holds Its Breath

As news of the Greenland invasion spread, the world's response was swift and fractured.

- NATO struggled to decide whether to respond militarily or politically.

- The European Union imposed immediate trade sanctions, though some leaders worried about economic fallout.
- China remained silent but watched closely.
- Russia quietly shifted its forces further into the Arctic.

And in Canada, Prime Minister Geneviève Lacroix sat in her office, watching it unfold.

Harland had proven that borders meant nothing.

And Canada, rich in resources, was right next door.

She knew what was coming.

The storm had begun.

And it would not end quietly.

PART I
LINES ARE DRAWN

1

THE ANNOUNCEMENT

Oval Office — Washington, D.C.

February 1, 2025
Nighttime

President Jefferson "Jeff" Harland sat behind the Resolute Desk, his fingers drumming against its polished oak surface. The desk, a relic of American history, had been crafted from the salvaged timbers of HMS Resolute, a British ship abandoned in the Arctic and later rescued by the United States. In gratitude, Queen Victoria had gifted it to President Rutherford B. Hayes in 1880, and since then, it had borne witness to the decisions that shaped the nation.

Tonight, it would bear witness again.

Harland was nothing like Hayes. Hayes had been a reformer, a man of integrity who fought corruption, championed civil service reform, and sought to protect the rights of Black Americans. He had lived modestly, opposed government excess, and carried himself with humility.

Jeff Harland was none of those things.

At seventy-five, he was broad-shouldered and heavyset, with a deep tan from endless golf outings and a signature mane of silver hair swept back like a man who wanted to be seen as larger than life. His small hands moved with the ease of a salesperson, his blue eyes cool and assessing, forever calculating the angles. His permanent smirk flickered between charm and menace, depending on his audience.

To Harland, democracy was not an ideal—it was an obstacle. A system bloated with unnecessary checks and balances, designed to restrain men like him. The Justice Department, the FBI, the inspectors general—all of them were bureaucratic parasites, meddling where they had no business. Oversight, accountability, transparency—these were the crutches of weak men. Harland had no use for them.

His vision was unshackled power, and his ambition was nothing short of imperial.

He saw America's greatness through himself, believing he was destined to reshape the world. He dreamed of annexing

Greenland, seizing the Panama Canal, and, ultimately, absorbing Canada itself. But he wasn't foolish. He wouldn't declare conquest outright. Instead, he draped his agenda in nationalism, wrapping his true intentions in the language of security, economic strength, and sovereignty.

He spoke of a war on drugs, of illegal immigrants flooding across the Canadian border, of foreign powers exploiting American goodwill. He spun historical distortions to plant the seeds of justification in the minds of his people. He did not see himself as just a president.

He saw himself as a conqueror.

And tonight, in his highly anticipated address to the nation, he would take the first step.

But first, he had a meeting.

The Triumvirate

With his inner circle, Harland never bothered with subtlety.

"That fucking bitch will retaliate with tariffs," he barked, referring to the Canadian Prime Minister.

He paced behind the desk, fists clenched.

"With our 25% tariffs on everything except their energy exports, Americans will feel it—twelve hundred dollars a person, I'm told. But if she hits back, I'll hit harder. I'll crush her."

Harland shouted most of the time. He was a bellicose bully, and in this room, he didn't bother pretending otherwise.

His Chief of Staff, Margaret "Maggie" Kellerman, didn't flinch. Sixty years old, tall, and skeletal, sharp-featured with deep wrinkles carved by stress and power, she had spent decades in Washington and had no patience for his tirades. Dressed in her signature dark pantsuit, she crossed her arms.

"Mr. President," she said, cool and measured. "You need to stop calling every woman who stands up to you a 'fucking bitch.' You're the President of the United States. Millions of women voted for you. And frankly, I find it disrespectful."

Harland reddened, his posture stiffening as he considered snapping back. But he had chosen Kellerman for a reason. She was brutal, fiercely loyal, and had delivered the Christian nationalist movement to his side. He needed her.

He exhaled, flexing his fingers.

"Fine," he muttered. "But she's still an annoying woman—person, whatever. I'd prefer dealing with the leader of the Opposition. He's weak. He'd be easier to break."

He turned to Garth Winthrop, the third member of the room.

"Have you started the purge?" Harland asked.

Winthrop, 48, slender, bald except for wisps of silver at the temples, with piercing green eyes and a perpetual smirk, barely looked up. He was the richest man in the world, powerful enough that even Harland tread carefully around him.

"Notices go out tomorrow," Winthrop replied smoothly. "We're terminating FBI officials hostile to the presidency and Justice Department lawyers who tried to prosecute you. They'll be replaced within a month. Law and order will be... redefined."

Harland nodded. Winthrop was the only man who dared speak to him this way. The President called it "our agenda."

Winthrop called it what it was. "My agenda."

Winthrop was the most dangerous man on Earth—a man who led the oligarchs, a class that corroded democracy worldwide for their own gain. He believed the poor were lazy, that the economy should be controlled by those who had already won, that the unqualified should have no say in the nation's direction.

These three were America's Triumvirate.

And they had a plan.

Storm

The Doctrine of Power

To achieve their vision, they would weaponize history.

- The Bush Doctrine gave them the precedent for preemptive war—if the U.S. could invade Iraq over a perceived threat, why not crush an economic rival the same way?
- The Roosevelt Corollary justified economic coercion—the U.S. had taken control of Latin America's economies for "stability" before. They could do it again.
- The Nixon Doctrine provided cover—America would support its allies while demanding they bend to its will.

With these blueprints, they did not need war to conquer.

They only needed to break the system and remake it in their image.

The First Strike

Harland pushed himself up from the desk. His silver hair gleamed under the soft light of the Oval Office.

"It's time," he said.

He straightened his tie, adjusted his smirk, and strode out of the room.

Tonight, he would declare economic war on Canada.

And it would be only the beginning.

Same Night

Ottawa, Ontario

She watched as the President addressed the American people, announcing a 25% tariff on all Canadian goods—except energy products, which would face a 10% tariff instead. That exception might serve as leverage down the road, but it was also a potential Achilles' heel. If Canada withheld energy exports, it could fracture the fragile united front forming against these tariffs.

The Prime Minister

Prime Minister Geneviève "Gen" Lacroix sat in her office in the West Block of Parliament Hill, watching the broadcast with her chief of staff.

The room was built for function and security, not for show. The old-style leather chairs were worn in places, softened by time, while Canadian artwork and historical artifacts lined the walls—subtle reminders of the country she had sworn to protect.

Lacroix had spent years practicing law in Montreal before entering politics, her sharp legal mind honed at Queen's University in Kingston. Now, instead of courtrooms and contracts, she dealt in power—negotiating, maneuvering, and, when necessary, drawing hard lines.

She carried herself with an air of quiet authority. Tall and fit, she moved with the confidence of someone who understood both her strengths and the weight of her position. Her wavy deep brown hair, streaked with silver at the temples, framed a face that rarely betrayed emotion. She was always impeccably dressed in tailored suits, not for vanity, but because she understood the unspoken language of politics—every detail mattered.

She was a strategist at heart, pragmatic and unflinching. Power, to her, was a tool, not an indulgence. She wielded it effectively in Canada's parliamentary system, knowing exactly when to push forward and when to hold back. A staunch defender of Canadian sovereignty, she wasn't afraid of confrontation, but she also understood the necessity of diplomacy.

In urban and progressive circles, she was respected as a leader who could keep the country united. In conservative and rural communities, she was often distrusted, seen as too detached from the everyday struggles of ordinary Canadians.

Despite the divisions at home, there was no disagreement on how to handle the crisis with Washington. The government and the opposition were, for once, in lockstep. So were the premiers.

But it was a fragile alliance. Every leader was watching the polls, waiting to see whether their constituents would support the battle that was about to unfold.

The Response

As the President's speech ended, Lacroix took a deep breath.

It was her turn now.

She stepped in front of the cameras for a late-night national address.

"Canada will not stand for an attack from a country that was supposed to be our friend and ally.

"Ottawa will immediately impose retaliatory tariffs on a range of American goods in response to President Harland's attempt to undermine the Canadian economy.

"To start, Canada will impose 25% tariffs on $30 billion worth of American goods beginning this Tuesday. An additional $125 billion in tariffs will be applied in three weeks.

"We did not ask for this fight. We do not want this fight. But we will not back down in defending Canadian jobs and industries."

She laid out the list of targeted American products—

- Liquor, beer, wine, and spirits
- Agricultural goods like vegetables and dairy
- Consumer products, from clothing to shoes to perfume
- Household goods, including appliances, furniture, and sports equipment

She urged Canadians to rally behind their country.

"Check the labels before you buy. Support Canadian businesses. Find your own way to stand up for Canada. In this moment, we must pull together—because we love this country."

President Harland had already warned that any retaliation would be met with even harsher measures.

Lacroix remained unshaken.

"We are not looking to escalate. But we will stand up for Canada, for Canadians, and for Canadian jobs. That is my responsibility—and that is exactly what we are doing."

She had tried to reach Harland since his inauguration two weeks ago.

He hadn't returned her calls.

But she wasn't giving up.

"The challenges we face—whether it's trade, security, or migration—should be tackled together as partners, not as adversaries.

"Canadians are upset. They are angry. And they have every right to be.

"But I have faith."

She let the last words linger, knowing they would be dissected, analyzed, and replayed across the country.

The speech was over.

The fight was just beginning.

2

FRIDAY BEERS AT HUSTLERS

Regina, Saskatchewan
February 6, 2025

Leonard "Lenny" Bishop sat on a high stool at Hustlers on South Albert Street, nursing a beer and enjoying the familiar banter of his five friends.

They called themselves The Bureaucrat Bunch—a half-joking, half-affectionate nod to their years of government service. Each of them had survived the bureaucratic labyrinth of the Saskatchewan government, navigating endless red tape and briefing notes.

Now retired, they spent their days critiquing the world and offering unsolicited advice on how to fix it—just as long as someone else did the actual fixing.

At 72, Lenny was the oldest of the group. Gaunt, gray-bearded, and wrapped in a weathered brown leather jacket that matched the creased skin on his face, he bore the marks of time and too many cigarettes.

- Years of smoking had left him with chronic lung issues.
- Arthritis nagged at his joints.
- Heart disease loomed over him like an unwelcome bureaucrat with a stack of paperwork.

But if anything, Lenny was stubborn—and he still enjoyed his beer, a little too much.

When he wasn't debating politics over drinks, he wrote crime novels—gritty, little-known thrillers that had gained him a modest but loyal following.

Sales were just enough to cover his publishing costs, but online, he was a bit of a social media guru. With active Facebook, Instagram, and LinkedIn accounts, he outpaced the rest of the Bureaucrat Bunch in tech-savviness—though that wasn't saying much.

In conversation, Lenny was sharp and witty, especially on political matters. But he preferred to let his writing do the real talking.

While his friends ranted, he sipped his beer, smirked, and listened.

Tariffs and Talk

Tonight's topic: Harland, tariffs, and the start of what some were calling an economic war.

Charlie, as usual, was holding court.

"Americans are nice one-on-one," he declared, slurring slightly. "But put 'em in a group, and suddenly they're shoving their way of life down everyone's throat."

It was a weak argument, considering the looming economic disaster for Canada, but no one called him on it.

Allan chimed in, slamming his fist on the table.

"We just can't let that jerk take our way of life from us!"

This led to more outrage, more indignant head-shaking, and a slew of half-baked ideas about what should be done—by someone younger, of course.

The prevailing sentiment: "We're too old for that shit."

Lenny smirked into his beer.

Retirement hadn't made them any less opinionated—just less motivated to do anything about it.

And really, that was just fine.

His friends trickled out, heading home to their wives, while Lenny lingered for one more beer.

There was no one waiting for him.

His wife had passed a few years earlier—cancer, the kind that took women too soon.

It happened fast.

She was gone and, in the ground, before he had fully grasped what it meant to be alone.

His two children had convinced him to sell their home in Albert Park and move into an apartment right behind Southland Mall.

"You'll be close to everything," they had reasoned. "You won't even need a car anymore."

But he held onto it anyway.

Giving up driving felt like giving up his freedom, and he was too stubborn for that.

On Friday nights, though, he walked.

Hustlers was just across the street, a short stroll from his apartment.

Walking meant he didn't have to care how many beers he had.

A Familiar Face

After finishing his drink, he left Hustlers and made his way home.

In the apartment elevator, he ran into his neighbor—Dr. Natalie Cheng.

A brilliant mind, at least in Lenny's opinion.

An economics professor at the University of Regina, she was much younger than he—38, if he remembered correctly.

He had thought of her in many ways:

- The Brainy Bachelorette
- The Thought Monk
- Dr. No-Nonsense

She looked the part—petite, with plain clothes draped over her slight frame, round glasses perched on her round face.

She was all intellect, no frills.

Yet, somehow, they had become friends.

Over time, they had fallen into an easy rhythm, sharing good whisky and sharp conversations about economics and politics.

Lenny had majored in economics in his undergraduate years —some fifty years ago—but it still fascinated him.

And, in a way, this friendship was enough.

Dinner Plans

"Natalie, have you eaten?" Lenny asked.

"No, Lenny. What do you have in mind?"

"Well, I had a few beers with the guys at Hustlers, and now I'm craving some Chinese. We could order in. I've got a bottle of Crown Royal Northern Harvest. What do you say?"

She smirked. "Sure, Lenny. It's not like my calendar is full."

So, they did just that—ordered in, ate Chinese, and sipped good whisky.

Rallying Behind Canada

As they ate, Natalie brought up the news.

"The Prime Minister is asking us to rally behind Canada."

"Yes, she did," Lenny replied, now teetering on the edge of tipsy. "Well, I'll tell you this—I'm never setting foot in the United States again. And piss on their beer, wine, and liquor."

Natalie raised an eyebrow. "Lenny, when was the last time you bought American beer, wine, or liquor?"

They both burst into laughter.

A Challenge

Then, shifting gears, Natalie said: "I have a meeting tomorrow afternoon with some colleagues—students, administrators, and a few community leaders. We'll be discussing ways individuals and organizations can make our retaliations more effective. I'd like you to join me."

Lenny scoffed. "Me? I'm just an old fart who writes shitty crime books to keep my mind busy. What could I contribute?"

Natalie studied him for a moment.

Was he really that unsure of his influence, or was he just looking for an excuse to avoid getting involved? She decided to push him.

"Lenny, you, and your cronies—and so many other seniors—act like you've done your part, like it's the younger generation's problem now. But let me tell you something—the younger generation is drowning.

"They're overwhelmed with jobs, kids, bills, and chasing whatever they think success is.

"They're disconnected from the reality you grew up with—when communism and nuclear war loomed over your heads, when your parents told you stories about World War II, about 50 million dead, about Germany and Japan's attempt to dominate the world.

"You lived through those lessons. You and your friends could be the ones leading this fight."

Lenny exhaled. "Oh, Natalie... I can barely breathe anymore."

She rolled her eyes.

"Look here, my friend—you breathe well enough to have written twenty-five books in the past five years, to go on radio talk shows promoting them, to attend book signings, to flood social media with your posts and ads.

"So don't bullshit me."

Lenny smirked, shaking his head.

And just like that, Natalie got her way.

3

PREMIERS' ZOOM MEETING

The tension in the virtual meeting was thick enough to cut with a knife.

Divisions in the Room

Premier Malcolm Rivers of Ontario sat at his desk, flipping through the briefing note in front of him. His jaw was set, his thick black hair slicked back as always. His signature red tie stood out against the dark navy suit.

Normally, he relished a fight—especially when it gave him a chance to rail against elites—but today, Ontario was bleeding, and he needed the other premiers to see that.

"Anti-American sentiment is rising fast," he said, his eyes sweeping across the faces on his screen. "These tariffs are hitting Ontario harder than anywhere else, and we need to act together."

Across the screen, Premier Travis Caldwell of Alberta shifted in his chair, arms crossed, his expression unreadable. Tall, rugged, and worn by years of ranching and backroom deals, Caldwell wasn't an easy man to move.

"I sympathize, Malcolm," he said, his voice slow, deliberate. "I do. But Alberta's already been fighting this battle for years. We warned you. We warned Ottawa. And now you want us to take a hit so Ontario can breathe easier?"

Rivers' lip curled.

"You think Alberta got off easy? You think a ten percent tariff on your biggest industry is a 'win'? Don't fool yourself, Travis. If this keeps up, investment in your oil sands will dry up, and you'll be dealing with layoffs too."

A Fractured Alliance

Eleanor Wong, Premier of British Columbia, sighed and unmuted herself. "Enough."

Her voice was calm but firm, a steadying force in the room.

"We're all taking damage. B.C.'s forestry sector is getting slaughtered. Our tech sector relies on U.S. contracts, and now those are at risk. If we start turning on each other, we're handing Washington the advantage."

Rivers nodded. "She's right. We need a Team Canada approach. We need to stand together, hit back as one."

That was when Premier François Ducharme of Quebec, who had been silent until now, leaned forward. "Then let's talk about the obvious play."

His French accent sharpened his words. "We hit them where it hurts. We cut the oil."

Caldwell's posture stiffened. "That's not happening."

Ducharme scoffed. "Why not? Alberta has the leverage. You say you don't like Ottawa dictating to you—fine. Then dictate to Washington. Let them feel what it's like to have their supply chain crippled."

Wong hesitated, then nodded. "If Alberta pauses energy exports for even a week, it could force Washington back to the table."

Caldwell's eyes darkened. "And throw Alberta into a full-blown economic crisis? I don't think so."

He turned to Rivers. "Ontario needs oil too, Malcolm. You ready for prices to skyrocket in your province? You ready for refineries to start shutting down?"

Rivers clenched his jaw. "I don't like it. But I also don't like sitting on my hands while thousands of Ontarian's lose their jobs."

Caldwell exhaled sharply; his frustration barely concealed. "You think Washington won't retaliate? That they won't find another way to punish us? You want me to blow up my province's economy for a gamble?"

Ducharme leaned in. "It's only a gamble if we don't commit."

Caldwell's fists tightened. "Easy for you to say. You don't have a damn thing to lose."

A long silence.

Wong rubbed her temples. "There has to be another way."

Rivers exhaled. "Then we need something just as strong. Something that will make Washington feel the pressure."

Caldwell was shaking his head before Rivers even finished speaking. "If you want Alberta to suffer so Ontario can have a better hand in negotiations, you're wasting your breath."

The meeting continued, but the divide was clear.

- Alberta wasn't going to shut off the taps.
- Ontario and Quebec weren't backing down.
- And Washington? They were watching, waiting for Canada to tear itself apart.

Economic Retaliation

The most significant news that came out of the Zoom call:

- Most of the Premiers were cutting off imports of wine, liquor, and beer from U.S. states that supported President Harland—referred to as the Red States.
- Premier Rivers and Premier Lemieux announced that government contracts with U.S. companies would be harder to get in their provinces.
- Premier Rivers added that Ontario had just canceled a million-dollar contract with a company owned by Garth Winthrop.

Prime Minister Lacroix Joins the Call

Prime Minister Geneviève Lacroix joined the Zoom call, her expression grave as she addressed the looming crisis.

"This is an existential threat from the United States."

The Saskatchewan Premier leaned forward, unfazed.

"American-made liquor will remain on my province's shelves," he declared. "Our economy depends on exports. If you and the Ontario Premier keep escalating this rhetoric, you'll only make things worse. We need to de-escalate, not inflame the situation."

His voice hardened. "And while we're at it, we need to dismantle interprovincial trade barriers. Frankly, those restrictions do more to stifle our growth than anything our southern neighbours are doing."

A tense silence filled the virtual room.

Then, Lacroix spoke. "I respect your concerns, Premier Annand, as I do those of everyone here. But together, we are far more formidable."

She let the words settle before adding, "And yes, I agree—interprovincial trade barriers must be addressed."

The Premier of New Brunswick broke in. "Prime Minister, Mexico has managed to get the U.S. to pause tariffs for a month. How?"

Lacroix's jaw tightened. "Mexico agreed to crack down on the border migrant crisis and fentanyl immediately. They've bought themselves time—one month to negotiate a more permanent arrangement."

Another Premier wasn't satisfied. "Then why can the Mexican President speak with President Harland and secure a pause, while you can't?"

Lacroix exhaled slowly. She knew the Premiers relished deflecting bad news onto her.

"Look," she said finally, "we've spent billions upgrading our border security, trying to placate Harland's demands. But the truth is, this was never about border security—it's political theatre, a distraction that plays well with his base.

"And there's another difference. Mexico isn't on his radar for expansion. We are.

"Mexico is fighting a trade war. We're fighting an attempted takeover."

The weight of her words hung heavy over the call.

More questions followed, and Lacroix answered them as best she could, her composure unwavering.

But before the debate could stretch further, an aide interrupted.

The Prime Minister was needed elsewhere.

The call ended.

And the crisis loomed larger than ever.

4

TRUE NORTH

A Gathering at the University

The meeting room in the University of Regina's economics department buzzed with quiet anticipation as chairs filled with professors, students, and local community members.

The early evening sunlight filtered through the tall windows, casting long shadows across the floor.

At the head of the room, Dr. Natalie Cheng, a well-respected professor of economics, stood confidently, reviewing her notes.

She had meticulously organized this gathering, ensuring that voices from across the country could be heard—whether in person or via live stream.

An Unlikely Attendee

Among those present was a man who had no idea why he had been asked to attend—Lenny Bishop.

A retired investigator with the Saskatchewan Auto Fund, Lenny had lived a life of structured routine since leaving the RCMP years ago. His past as an undercover officer in Vancouver and Toronto was known to very few, and he preferred it that way.

It had been a lengthy career, filled with secrets and dangers he had long since left behind. Yet here he was, sitting among scholars and activists, pulled into something he didn't yet understand, all because his neighbor and friend, Dr. Cheng, had urged him to come.

Natalie Takes the Stage

As the last few attendees settled, Cheng stepped to the podium and tapped the microphone.

"Thank you all for being here tonight. Whether you're from Saskatchewan or tuning in from across Canada, welcome."

She scanned the room, her eyes resting for a moment on Lenny.

"We have a special guest tonight."

"A brilliant writer of true and fictional crime stories, someone who knows how to reach audiences—particularly the 50-plus demographic. I believe his skills may be invaluable to our cause."

She gestured toward Lenny.

"Please welcome Lenny Bishop."

A polite round of applause rippled through the room.

Lenny forced a nod of acknowledgment. He wasn't sure what Cheng meant by "our cause," but he had a feeling he was about to find out.

The Birth of a Movement

Cheng pressed on.

"True North, Strong and Free—TNSF—was born out of a need to protect Canadian sovereignty.

"We are here because of what's happening to our economy and what may happen if Harland wins the U.S. Presidential election.

"We have seen the threats—American policies designed to weaken our industries, to exploit our resources, to make us dependent. We refuse to stand by and let it happen."

A murmur of agreement swept through the crowd.

Lenny watched as students nodded passionately, and community leaders whispered among themselves. He noted the presence of representatives from First Nations and Métis governments, food banks, and other social organizations.

This wasn't just an economic think tank—It was a movement.

Cheng continued:

"Over the last three months, we've been organizing across the country. Tonight, we will hear reports from each region on their efforts.

"Our mission is simple: we inform Canadians on how to keep their wealth in Canada.

"Buy Canadian.

"Sell off American stocks, bonds, and properties.

"Pressure our governments to protect our industries and disengage from the U.S. economy where possible.

"This is economic resistance."

Lenny shifted in his seat. This was radical.

Not in a reckless way—everything sounded legal, at least so far—but it was clear that TNSF aimed to strike back at the U.S. in a way that could have real consequences.

A Watchful Eye

As Cheng invited the first regional representative to speak, Lenny's gaze drifted across the room.

He had been trained to read people, to look for the outlier, the person who didn't quite fit.

And then he saw him—Someone who looked just a little too polished, a little too interested in taking notes rather than participating.

Unbeknownst to everyone in the room, a young man posing as a student sat quietly at the back, taking careful notes.

His real identity? A CIA operative, embedded to monitor the growing movement.

Washington had already taken notice of TNSF, and they wanted to gauge just how far this group was willing to go.

As regional updates continued, a deep unease settled over Lenny. He wasn't sure what he had walked into, but one thing was clear—This was more than just a debate about Canadian economics. It was a battle for sovereignty.

And somehow, he had just been pulled into the front lines.

The Aftermath

Once the formal meeting ended, the room relaxed into casual discussions.

Lenny followed Natalie as she moved through the crowd, introducing him to professors and students who had participated in the evening's discussions.

He shook hands, nodded at names he would never remember, and smiled politely as each person greeted him with the same line: "I wasn't aware of your books."

He gave them all the same answer: "You can find them on Amazon."

But in the back of his mind, a bitter thought surfaced—*Of course, they haven't heard of me. I'm not a brilliant writer. My books are self-published and not in mainstream bookstores.*

Natalie, unfazed, continued her introductions, guiding Lenny from the academic circles to the community representatives.

Among them were Indigenous leaders and advocates from food banks and shelters—People working on the ground, preparing for the economic fallout they believed was coming.

Lenny listened as they spoke of their concerns, strategies, and hopes.

The more he heard, the more he realized—This wasn't just intellectual posturing. These people were planning for something real.

And as much as he had told himself he was just here as a favor to Natalie, a part of him knew—He was already in too deep to walk away.

An Evening Drive

Finally, it was over, Lenny told himself as Natalie stood up, announcing that she was going to get her winter coat and boots. She had driven them to the meeting, and he was more than ready to head home.

Outside, the cold Saskatchewan air bit at their faces as they climbed into Natalie's 1968 Mercedes-Benz. The old car took a few minutes to warm up, its engine rumbling as frost melted from the windshield.

Natalie was a bit eccentric, but Lenny had always figured university types were.

"Lenny let's stop at Roots Kitchen for a bite and a drink," she said, turning onto the road.

A Proposition at Roots Kitchen

"Sure, Natalie. Another night where my calendar is wide open," he replied dryly.

Seated at a corner table in the cozy restaurant, Lenny sensed that Natalie had more on her mind than just dinner.

It wasn't long before she laid her cards on the table.

"I want to recruit you," she said. "You're a senior, and seniors have economic power that can put real pressure on the U.S."

Lenny raised an eyebrow, and Natalie continued.

"Canadian Snowbirds represent a significant economic force in the United States, especially in Florida, Arizona, and Texas, where they own or rent properties for months at a time.

"Their spending supports real estate, rental markets, retail, and tourism-based businesses. From dining and shopping to entertainment and recreation, Snowbirds pump billions into the U.S. economy each year.

"Their collective purchasing power makes them an influential force, shaping regional economic trends. If they changed their habits—even a little—it could have real consequences."

Lenny leaned back and smirked. "But why me, Natalie? I could drop dead on you right now. I'm an old bird."

Natalie smiled. "Because we're friends and neighbours. I can drop by anytime and keep you updated with key messaging. And you know social media marketing. You already have a base—even if it's small, it's bigger than almost anyone else in Regina your age. You'll be able to connect with others across Canada."

Lenny tapped his fingers on the table, then looked up and said, "Natalie, did you know there was a spy in the room today?"

Natalie laughed. "Oh? And how would you know, Lenny? Were you some kind of Canadian spook in your younger years?"

Lenny didn't laugh. He just sipped his drink, considering his next move. Then, after a long pause, he nodded. "Alright. I'll do it."

The Growing Storm

Lenny switched on his television the moment he stepped into his apartment, the familiar blue glow filling the dim room.

He flipped to The National on CBC—the late-night news—a ritual he rarely skipped.

The lead story was impossible to ignore.

Canada's response to the American tariffs had been swift and visceral.

- Across the country, hockey arenas erupted in boos whenever the U.S. national anthem played.
- Social media was ablaze—Facebook was flooded with Canadians announcing they'd canceled vacations to the States.
- Twitter and Instagram were plastered with lists of homegrown brands, urging citizens to "Buy Canadian."

- More dramatically, reports surfaced of Canadians withdrawing their money from U.S. banks, a silent but deliberate protest against their closest ally.

The news anchor's voice was measured but firm. "Canadians are feeling disrespected and betrayed by their neighbor to the south."

Then, the segment shifted to reactions from across the border.

"The new 25% tariff on Canadian imports is sparking debate in the U.S. A Harris poll shows two-thirds of Americans expect higher prices, with business leaders warning of job losses and supply chain disruptions.

"While some support the move as a step toward revitalizing American manufacturing, others fear it will lead to retaliation and economic fallout.

"For now, uncertainty looms as consumers and industries brace for the impact."

Lenny exhaled heavily. A part of him believed he was insulated from all this.

He hadn't set foot in the U.S. since his wife passed. As far as he knew, his purchases were all Canadian—Hell, at least his beer was.

His books were sold on Amazon, but that hardly counted, did it? He was a Canadian writer, selling to Canadian readers. He had read somewhere that Amazon used Canadian printers to reduce costs. Surely, that meant he was in the clear.

Still, the unease lingered.

"Oh, Natalie is persuasive."

With that thought gnawing at him, Lenny turned off the television and crawled into bed, his mind as unsettled as the storm brewing between the two nations.

5

AMERICAN POWER

The War Council Assembles

President Jefferson Harland leaned back in the grand leather chair of the Oval Office, taking a slow, deliberate look around.

He had spent his career in power, but nothing compared to this—the unmatched authority of being President of the United States.

Everything within this room, from the weight of history to the men before him, was a reminder of his dominion.

The Men Who Ran America

To his right stood General Randal Lutz, 62, a barrel-chested relic of old-school American militarism.

His crew-cut gray hair, jagged scar on his cheek, and cold, unreadable stare reminded Harland of General Jack D. Ripper from *Dr. Strangelove*. In the film, the unhinged Air Force general had plunged the world into nuclear war—Lutz wasn't far off.

And that was precisely why Harland had appointed him as Chairperson of the Joint Chiefs of Staff.

Across from him sat Dale Carver, FBI Director, 58.

He was broad-shouldered, weathered from a life under the Arizona sun. A thick moustache and ever-present cowboy boots gave him the look of a man who still believed in frontier justice.

To the country, he was "Sheriff Dave," a tough-on-crime legend who had ruled Maricopa County for years.

Civil rights groups called his methods unconstitutional—Harland called them necessary.

Carver had been handpicked for one reason: To purge the FBI of "woke" influences.

Since taking over the Bureau, he had redirected counterterrorism resources—no longer focusing on foreign threats or organized crime, but instead targeting activists, journalists, and "leftist agitators."

His enemies weren't cartel bosses or domestic terrorists—They were intellectuals, the press, and anyone who questioned American supremacy.

Harland's icy blue eyes shifted again, settling on his Chief of Intelligence, Colonel Trent Vickers, 45.

- Stocky, buzz-cut dark hair, a strong jaw.
- Always in military fatigues, even in government meetings.
- A former helicopter pilot, risen through the ranks with one belief: "Intelligence isn't for gathering information—it's for eliminating threats."

Vickers saw himself as a warrior, not a bureaucrat.

He distrusted career politicians, despised academics, and viewed traditional intelligence protocols as outdated relics of a weaker America.

Then there was Victor Langston, the newly appointed Attorney General, 64.

A heavyset, disheveled figure, whose thick, graying hair and ever-present five o'clock shadow made him look more like a war strategist than a lawyer.

A former media executive turned legal bulldog; Langston thrived on chaos. He saw the Department of Justice as a weapon, not an institution.

His first act as Attorney General?

- Refocus the DOJ on "real threats"—activists, journalists, and federal watchdogs.
- Launch antitrust investigations against tech companies accused of censoring conservatives.
- Cut funding to universities, which he deemed indoctrination centres.
- Crack down on sanctuary cities, ensuring they would soon face direct federal intervention.

The law, under Langston, wasn't about justice—It was about control.

Harland's Vision

Harland clasped his hands together, surveying the room.

This was his team—his war council. They weren't restrained by politics, diplomacy, or morality. They were men who understood power and were willing to wield it.

And yet, there was something familiar about them.

The way they dressed.

The way they carried themselves.

The way they spoke in clipped, decisive tones.

It was as if the past had reached into the present—A meeting that could have taken place under Eisenhower or Nixon.

The only difference? They weren't just remembering the past —They were trying to bring it back.

The CIA Report

Vickers spoke first, handling the CIA report.

Prior to Harland's election, covert plans had been drafted to begin CIA operations in Canada—Without the knowledge of the Canadian government.

This wouldn't be the first time.

- It had been exposed during the Edward Snowden affair that the U.S. operated freely on Canadian soil, exploiting Canada's intelligence networks.

The Snowden Precedent

Edward Snowden, a former NSA contractor, had leaked classified documents in 2013, exposing global mass surveillance programs conducted by the NSA and its allies, including Canada's CSE, under the Five Eyes intelligence-sharing alliance.

His disclosures revealed:

- Widespread monitoring of citizens, foreign leaders, and corporations.
- Illegal surveillance operations.
- Exploitation of Canada's intelligence networks by the U.S.

His revelations had led to:

- •International outrage.
- •Debates over privacy and government overreach.
- •Surveillance law reforms—but no real change in how intelligence was used.

Snowden had fled prosecution in the U.S., ultimately finding asylum in Russia.

To some, he was a whistleblower. To others, he was a traitor.

Targeting Canada

Now, Vickers had implemented new measures.

He had ordered operatives to infiltrate Canadian universities, believing that the most radical Canadians would be professors and students.

Today, he reported a growing network of individuals and organizations joining what was becoming known as:

True North, Strong and Free (TNSF), an underground movement forming in opposition to U.S. influence.

Harland's Directive

The President leaned forward. "What measures are you taking?"

Vickers shrugged. "It's loosely tied together for now. Nothing significant that threatens our national interests. We have our people in place to monitor their activities. For now, I recommend watching and reporting."

Harland nodded.

Then he turned to his FBI Director. "Dale, what's happening on the home front?"

The Domestic Crackdown

Carver snickered. "Dismissal letters are being issued as we speak to 4,000 FBI agents who we believe will passively resist your agenda.

"We're placing surveillance on them to determine if and how they might try to undermine us."

Harland smirked. "Good."

The Bear in the Room: Victor Langston

Then there was the bear in the room—Victor Langston.

The Attorney General leaned forward, his heavy hands folded on the table, his voice a gravelly growl as he outlined his progress.

"Liberal DOJ staff are being purged. Funding for progressive police reform is gone, replaced by grants for rearming and militarizing law enforcement.

"The media? We've applied enough pressure to get key journalists fired and force a shift in coverage. Those reporters who kept attacking you, Mr. President, are out."

He exhaled, savouring the moment.

"Thousands of January 6th prisoners have been released. And federal oversight agencies? Gutted.

"Meanwhile, we've moved aggressively against leftist movements, including Antifa. Their protests, their agitators, their social networks—everything is under scrutiny.

"The message is clear: resistance has consequences."

The President's War Council

Harland let his eyes drift around the room, taking in the faces of his inner circle.

He had chosen these men carefully.

They were warriors.

And this was a war.

6

CALM BEFORE THE STORM

The Weight of Uncertainty

Lenny awoke on Monday morning, February 9, 2025, two days after the TNSF gathering at the university.

He had met Natalie that night, and ever since, an uneasy feeling gnawed at him.

He had spent all of Sunday fretting over what she had dragged him into.

He hadn't done anything yet—hadn't even received any marching orders—but he could already feel the weight of something bigger than himself pressing down.

And then there was the matter of the so-called spy.

His gut told him he was right—someone had been in that room, collecting intelligence.

That instinct had served him well in his years as an undercover cop, but now, at seventy-two, long retired, could he still trust his gut?

A Visit to RCMP Headquarters

By mid-morning, he had made his decision.

He would go straight to Saskatchewan RCMP Headquarters on Dewdney Avenue.

He knew the right man to talk to—Inspector Ron McDavid, the province's key contact for RCMP National Security.

A single phone call was all it took—McDavid agreed to meet him immediately.

Lenny Bishop wasn't just another retired Mountie. He was a legend.

The Meeting with McDavid

McDavid greeted him in the lobby, a broad, calloused hand extended in welcome.

He was a brute of a man—muscles pushing against his RCMP officer's uniform, his presence commanding.

- Clean-shaven.
- Square-jawed.
- Strikingly handsome.

Lenny, by contrast, looked every bit the weathered veteran.

Softening was a generous way to describe how time had reshaped his once-imposing frame.

The handshake was firm, measuring.

"Inspector," Lenny said.

"Mr. Bishop," McDavid replied, leading him down the hall.

Inside McDavid's office, Lenny got straight to the point. He recounted what had happened at the TNSF gathering, watching the younger officer's face for a reaction.

McDavid nodded. "We know all about them."

"Then you also know there was a spy in that room," Lenny said.

McDavid didn't flinch. "It wasn't one of ours."

Lenny smirked. "I'd have known if it was."

McDavid studied him carefully, his expression unreadable.

"We've got several far-right groups in Saskatchewan that despise organizations like TNSF. Maybe one of them sent someone?"

Lenny didn't smirk this time. His expression shifted—less amusement, more weight.

"Inspector," he said, his voice lowering, "since I retired, I've kept my distance. No alumni events, no war stories, no cozy reunions. I don't talk about my time as a Mountie because I broke a lot of rules. I played dirty when I had to.

"Undercover work wasn't clean, and I never wanted to be dragged in front of a Royal Commission or an RCMP inquiry, forced to admit to the things I did to stop terrorism, to dismantle organized crime."

He leaned in slightly. "The man in that room wasn't some redneck from a right-wing fringe group. He was CIA."

McDavid's expression hardened.

"Short hair. Taking notes. Fixating on speakers—memorizing their faces. Smart. Too smart to be some local thug. And, Inspector, this wouldn't be the CIA's first time operating illegally in Canada.

"They were here during Vietnam, spying on draft dodgers. After 9/11, they tracked our Muslim communities. You know as well as I do that, they don't respect borders—not when they think their interests are at stake."

McDavid took a moment to process.

When he finally spoke, his voice was careful but firm. "Mr.

Bishop, I'll report this to National Security and CSIS. Can we keep you in the loop?"

Lenny hesitated. The last thing he wanted was to get pulled back in. And he sure as hell wasn't going to be their informant inside the TNSF.

Finally, he nodded. "Only you contact me, McDavid. No one else. And you don't ask about TNSF."

McDavid held his gaze, then extended his hand again. "Agreed." They shook on it.

Lenny left without looking back.

The Assignment

A Quiet Café, A Loud Proposition

Lenny watched the steam curl from his coffee, the aroma rich and familiar. Across from him, Natalie Cheng studied him over the rim of her cup, her sharp eyes assessing, measuring.

They had met at a quiet corner cafe in downtown Regina, a place where conversations faded into the hum of espresso machines and the clinking of spoons. The kind of spot where people who didn't want to be overheard chose to meet.

Lenny leaned back in his chair; arms crossed. "Alright, Natalie. You dragged me into that TNSF meeting. Now tell me—what exactly do you want from me?"

Natalie set her cup down with deliberate care, folding her hands together. Then she smiled—a small, knowing smile. "Lenny, you have presence. When you talk, people listen. They trust you."

He frowned. "That's a hell of a setup for a favor. Your flattery won't work on me."

Natalie chuckled. "It's not flattery, and it's not a favor. It's more than that. In three months, TNSF will have you very well known."

Lenny's eyes narrowed. "And why's that?"

"Because there aren't many 72-year-old men writing and self-publishing successfully. Your books sell to an audience you built yourself. You created that market through your own efforts."

Lenny exhaled, rubbing his temple. "I barely break even. It's a hobby, not a movement. But go on."

Natalie leaned in now, her expression hardening. "We're at war, Lenny. Not with bullets. Not with tanks. With money."

Lenny scoffed. "What, you mean the usual? The U.S. squeezing us dry, bullying us into bad trade deals?"

Natalie's voice was quiet but firm. "No. Worse than that. They're not just pushing their agenda through governments and corporations anymore.

"They're going after individual Canadians—one by one. And seniors are their easiest targets."

The True Target

Lenny's brow furrowed. "Seniors? I thought this was just about buying Canadian and skipping vacations in the States. You're saying it's bigger than that?"

Natalie nodded. "Much bigger. Seniors hold billions in fixed incomes, pensions, and assets. That wealth makes them vulnerable.

"Pensions can be undermined. Savings manipulated. And a lot of them own property in the U.S. What's stopping federal and state governments down there from hiking foreign ownership fees? From slapping massive capital gains taxes on Canadian retirees when they try to sell?"

She shook her head. "This isn't static, Lenny. The methods change as needed. Don't be naïve."

Lenny took a slow sip of coffee, considering. "And what exactly do you want me to do about it?"

"I want you to educate them."

Lenny laughed—sharp and short. "Me? I'm no economist. You've got the brains at TNSF. Get them to do it."

Natalie's voice remained even. "They already built the system. A social media network—specifically designed to reach seniors. To inform them about what's really happening. To teach them how to fight back economically."

Lenny shook his head. "Then use them. What do you need me for?"

Natalie's gaze locked onto his. "Because they won't listen to me. Or to some young economist throwing around theories. But they'll listen to you."

She paused, letting the words settle. "You're real, Lenny. No nonsense. Grounded. They trust people like you."

The Role of a Leader

Lenny exhaled through his nose, rubbing his temple. "So, what? You want me to be your spokesperson?"

"No," Natalie corrected. "I want you to be a leader. Someone they can look to for guidance. Someone who understands what's at stake."

Lenny traced the rim of his cup, thinking. "And what exactly is at stake, Natalie?"

She held his gaze. "Independence."

A beat of silence passed between them.

"They want us dependent," she went on. "On their banks. Their policies. Their corporations.

"The moment we start protecting our own wealth, investing in ourselves, breaking free of their control—they lose power.

"And trust me, Lenny, they won't let that happen without a fight."

The Proof

Lenny mulled it over, his skepticism clear.

Natalie pulled out her phone, swiped through an article, and slid it across the table. "Look at this."

Lenny squinted at the headline: Canadian Pension Funds at Risk as Foreign Investors Flood Market.

He frowned, scrolling through the text. "They're selling off pension-backed assets to foreign buyers…"

"Exactly," Natalie said. "Corporations with American interests are quietly buying up Canada's retirement security.

"What happens when they decide to cash out? When they raise rates? Seniors lose their pensions overnight. And that's just one angle."

Lenny's grip on the phone tightened. "Jesus."

Natalie wasn't finished. "There's more. Banks steering seniors into high-risk investments, knowing they'll crash. Policies stripping away protections for older Canadians.

"We can fight back, but only if people know what's happening."

Lenny placed the phone back on the table, looking at Natalie, his gut twisting. "You're asking me to wake up a sleeping army."

Natalie smiled. "I knew you'd get it."

Lenny let out a slow breath, staring into his coffee.

He didn't like the spotlight.

Didn't like playing the role of a leader.

But if Natalie was right—and his gut told him she was—then Canada's seniors were walking blind into an economic trap.

And if he could stop it...

He exhaled, nodding slowly. "I'm in."

Natalie grinned. "Good. Let's get to work."

PART II

MEASURES TAKE EFFECT

JUNE 2025

7

ONTARIO'S ECONOMY IS SUFFERING

Phone Call: Prime Minister Geneviève Lacroix and Ontario Premier Malcolm Rivers

Prime Minister Geneviève "Gen" Lacroix pressed the phone against her ear, listening as Ontario Premier Malcolm Rivers tore into her.

His voice was raw with frustration—the kind that came from leading a province teetering on the edge of disaster. "You wanted retaliation? Well, we got it," Rivers growled. "And guess what? It's not working."

Gen exhaled slowly, pinching the bridge of her nose.

The 25% counter-tariff Canada had slapped on American imports was supposed to send a message. Instead, the message coming back was clearer, louder, and a hell of a lot uglier than expected.

"The reports are still coming in, Malcolm," she said, keeping her voice even. "It's too early to say the tariffs aren't working. We're still analyzing—"

"No, Gen." His tone was sharp, cutting. "I don't need your analysts to tell me what I already know. I see it on the ground, every goddamn day. Businesses shutting down. Supply chains in chaos. Consumer prices through the roof."

"We knew there would be short-term pain," she countered.

Rivers let out a bitter laugh. "Short-term? It's been five months. Where's the payoff? Where's the American retreat? Because from where I'm standing, all I see is Ontario getting crushed."

The Numbers Don't Lie

Gen shut her eyes. She didn't need Rivers to paint the picture—she had seen the numbers herself.

- Food imports from the U.S. had plunged by 40%—but instead of boosting domestic agriculture, it had sent grocery prices spiralling up another 9%.
- Retail sectors were collapsing as big-box stores buckled under skyrocketing costs.

- Manufacturers were cutting shifts as American components became too expensive to import, while domestic suppliers couldn't scale up fast enough.

She had fought to keep these numbers out of the press—for now.

But Rivers wasn't wrong. The pain was real.

A Desperate Option

"I know what's happening, Malcolm," she said quietly. "I've got a team working on a relief package—"

"A bailout?" he cut in. "Like you did during the pandemic?"

Gen hesitated. She hadn't spoken publicly about it yet. Canadians were still reeling from the inflationary fallout of the COVID-era stimulus.

Another massive spending package could send inflation spiralling again. But at this rate, She might not have a choice. "I'm considering it," she admitted.

"Well, consider faster."

She clenched her jaw. "It's not that simple, Malcolm. If we pour billions into a bailout, we risk triggering another inflationary spiral when recovery kicks in and demand outpaces production.

"And you know as well as I do, the Bank of Canada can't keep hiking interest rates without pushing people into financial ruin. It can't just flood the economy with money if we aren't producing enough goods and services to match."

Silence.

Then, Rivers spoke again—lower this time, the anger replaced with something heavier. "They're already broken, Gen."

His voice was almost quiet now. "You think interest rates are what's keeping people up at night? Try job losses. Try seniors watching their pensions evaporate because U.S. corporations are gutting our investments. Try families who can't afford groceries because of the very tariffs you signed off on."

Gen rubbed her temple.

Political Reality

The economic reports were bad.

The political ones were worse.

Public approval of her government was tanking. The opposition members were circling like vultures, calling the trade war a catastrophic failure.

"We don't have the fiscal space for a massive bailout, Malcolm," she said carefully.

"Then find the damn space."

"It's not that easy."

"Nothing about this is easy, Gen." Rivers' voice sharpened. "I don't care about your political calculus or your talking points. I care about the three thousand auto workers in Windsor and Oshawa who are out of a job.

"The thousands of small businesses barely hanging on. You want to keep playing chicken with the Americans? Fine. But you better have a plan to keep Ontario from hitting the pavement."

Gen's grip on the phone tightened. "You think I don't know what's at stake?" she shot back. "I see the same damn numbers you do. And if we don't hold the line, we'll be signing away what little economic independence we have left."

Silence.

Then, Rivers exhaled. "I get it," he said finally. "You're looking at the big picture. But I need you to see mine."

His voice softened, but the urgency never faded. "Ontario is burning, Gen. You don't have months to figure this out. You don't even have weeks."

Gen pressed her lips together. He was right. Five months in, they were losing control.

And if she didn't act soon, it wouldn't just be Ontario on the brink—It would be all of Canada.

She took a slow breath. "You'll have an answer in a week."

"You've got five days."

Click. The line went dead.

Gen stared at the phone in her hand. Five days.

She turned to her desk. The bailout proposal sat untouched at the top of the pile.

No Other Choice

She hadn't wanted to pull the trigger on it—but after this call, she knew one thing for certain. She might not have a choice.

Prime Minister Geneviève Lacroix's Address to the Nation

"A Call to Strength, Sacrifice, and Sovereignty"

[Live National Broadcast]

Opening Words

My fellow Canadians. Tonight, I come before you not just as your Prime Minister, but as a Canadian—One who loves this country One who believes in its people.

One who knows that when faced with great challenges, we do not falter. We rise.

Acknowledging the Crisis

Over the past five months, our nation has endured an economic assault unlike anything we have seen before.

A 25% tariff, imposed on us by a foreign power, has sent shockwaves through our economy.

We answered forcefully, imposing our own tariffs in return. But trade wars are never painless.

- Our businesses.
- Our workers.
- Our families.

All are feeling the strain.

Some have lost jobs. Some have closed businesses they spent a lifetime building. Many are seeing the cost of everyday goods rise and are wondering how much more they can endure.

The Reason We Fight

Let me be clear: This was not a fight we sought, but it is a fight we must win.

Our economic independence—

- Our ability to control our own industries.

- To protect our workers.

- To keep our wealth within Canada.

All are at stake. And I promise you, we will not surrender.

A Bold Response: The National Economic Stabilization Plan

Tonight, your government is taking a bold and decisive action. We are launching the National Economic Stabilization Plan—an emergency effort to protect workers, businesses, and families from the worst effects of this economic war.

This plan will provide:

- Direct financial support to workers.
- Relief for small businesses.
- Investment in domestic industries.
- Protection for our pension system.

The Role of Every Canadian

But my fellow Canadians, government action alone is not enough.

If we are to win this fight, it will take strength and sacrifice from every one of us. For some, that will mean paying more to buy Canadian. For others, it will mean cutting back, adapting, standing firm.

A History of Resilience

History has tested us before.

- In war.
- In recession.
- In crisis.

Canadians have never broken. And we will not break now.

We do not back down. We do not walk away from a fight when our future is at stake.

We fight smarter. We stand stronger. And we move forward together.

Closing Words

May we stand united, And may Canada always stand free.

[Broadcast Ends]

8

THE MADE-UP LEADER

TNSF Takes Over

True North Strong and Free (TNSF) had exploded into a national force, commanding millions of subscribers.

The movement's $50 annual membership fee alone generated a steady flood of funding, while business and individual donations ensured that TNSF's war chest was full.

With money came strategy, and TNSF spared no expense in making Lenny Bishop a household name.

Lenny had maxed out his 5,000 Facebook (META) friend limit, but that was only the beginning.

Many of his friends had their own maxed-out networks, meaning that when Lenny posted something, it spread like wildfire—Reaching over 20 million people across Canada and the U.S. with every major update.

The First Major Post

Then came the first major post—a simple explanation of the Canadian government's retaliatory 25% tariff—why grocery prices were rising, and how it was hitting every household.

> WHY ARE GROCERY PRICES RISING?
>
> UNDERSTANDING CANADA'S 25% TARIFF ON U.S. IMPORTS

By Lenny Bishop, TNSF

> HOW DOES THIS AFFECT YOU?

- Many of the products we buy—fruits, vegetables, packaged foods, and other essentials—come from the U.S.
- With the tariff, Canadian businesses must pay more to bring these products into the country.
- Stores pass those extra costs onto shoppers, making groceries more expensive.

> WHY NOT JUST BUY CANADIAN?

While some foods are grown in Canada, we still rely on U.S. imports—especially in winter. Finding local alternatives takes time, and Canadian farmers cannot always increase supply overnight.

BOTTOM LINE:
The tariff was meant to pressure the U.S. in a trade dispute, but in the short term, it's making life more expensive for Canadian families.

CALL TO ACTION:
Let's talk—what changes have you noticed in grocery prices?

Have you changed your shopping habits to rally for Canada's sovereignty?

The Viral Impact

The call to action worked. Millions of Canadians flooded the comments, message boards, and discussion forums, sharing personal stories about their growing grocery bills.

TNSF gained critical intel—not just on the economic toll, but on how people were thinking and responding.

Even Americans weighed in. Many were sympathetic—but some fired back with anger, resentment, and mockery.

The Post That Set the Country on Fire

Then came the post that set the country on fire.

> TIME TO SELL: WHY CANADIAN SNOWBIRDS SHOULD GET OUT NOW
>
> By Lenny Bishop, for TNSF
>
> THE PROBLEM
>
> For years, Canadian retirees have enjoyed winters in the U.S., owning properties in Florida, Arizona, and beyond.
> But that golden era is ending—And if you own U.S. property, now is the time to sell and get out before it costs you even more.
>
> WHAT'S CHANGING?
>
> The U.S. is tightening financial screws on foreign property owners.
>
> - Property taxes are rising.
> - New foreign ownership fees are on the table.
> - Washington could increase capital gains taxes on Canadian sellers at any time.

Meanwhile,

The Canadian dollar is at historic lows. Every dollar spent in the U.S. now costs significantly more.

But when you sell your U.S. home, those American dollars convert into a whole lot of Canadian money.

WHY SELL NOW?

✔ Cash out while your property still holds value—before a wave of sales floods the market.
✔ Take advantage of the U.S.-Canada exchange rate—your sale proceeds will be worth far more back home.
✔ Avoid higher costs and taxes before Washington decides to take even more from Canadian owners.
✔ Reinvest in Canada—where your money benefits you, not a country that sees you as a convenient cash source.

The Fallout Was Instant

Snowbirds who hadn't even considered selling were now defending their choices or feeling pressure from friends, family, and neighbours who questioned their loyalty to Canada's cause.

TNSF leaders watched the numbers closely.

If even a fraction of Canadian-owned U.S. properties hit the market, it could set off a chain reaction that would send the American housing market into a tailspin.

Natalie's Perspective

Natalie watched Lenny as the movement gained momentum and division at the same time.

TNSF was winning, but the battlefield was changing.

The Reality of War

"It's just an example of what happens when a country is at war," she told him.

"England saw the same thing during the Second World War. Not every citizen shared the same interests, and patriotic duty meant different things to different people. It created tensions, resentment, even betrayal among neighbours."

She gave him a small, knowing smile. "It's unavoidable, Lenny."

A Familiar Shadow

Hustlers Bar – Regina, Saskatchewan

It was a warm Friday in June, and the guys were gathering for beers at Hustlers.

Lenny hadn't been a regular in weeks. Between radio and TV interviews, podcasts, and community meetings across Saskatchewan, his time had been consumed by TNSF.

He had flat-out refused their push for him to travel across Canada. "You can find some old farts in other provinces to do that," he had told them.

Tonight, though, he needed this—needed to sit with people who weren't looking at him through a camera lens, people who knew him before all this began.

The Welcome of Old Friends

The guys were already deep into their drinks; one seat sat open for him at their usual table. As he approached, they hooted and hollered, some even standing and bowing in exaggerated gestures. "Look at this! The man, the myth, the legend!"

Lenny rolled his eyes and took his seat. "Fuck off," he said, shaking his head as they laughed.

The teasing settled, and conversation flowed—

- Work gripes.
- Hockey.
- Some poor bastard's bad luck in the markets.

Lenny listened, sipping his beer, realizing something. No one was talking about the trade war. It wasn't avoidance—it was exhaustion.

He figured the meetings he'd missed had drained the topic dry. They didn't ask him about it, and he didn't bring it up.

Then, out of habit, he scanned the room.

Eyes on a Ghost

His gaze landed on a booth to his left—And there he was.

- Same sharp blue eyes.
- Same too-casual posture.
- Same kid from the university gathering with Natalie.

The kid was trying too hard to avoid eye contact—which meant he knew Lenny had spotted him.

Lenny set his beer down, rose from his chair, and walked over. The young man didn't flinch as Lenny slid into the seat across from him. He simply smiled, that same calm, calculating expression on his face.

The Conversation Begins

"Mr. Bishop, or can I just call you Lenny?" His voice was smooth, casual but watchful. "You've become well known very quickly. What can I do for you?"

Lenny studied him for a beat, then leaned in slightly. "First off, I need to know what I should call you. Just the name the CIA has you using for your illegal surveillance in my country."

A slight smirk. No surprise. No denial.

"Mmm, I expected the legendary Lenny Bishop might make me," the young man said, tilting his head slightly. "My name is Ethan Cole. It's my real name, and I'm in Canada legally on a temporary student visa, working toward my master's in political science."

A pause.

"The fact that I'm on leave from my employer to obtain that degree and the fact that I happen to be in the same bar as you does not make me an illegal operative in Canada."

His blue eyes held steady, his tone light but firm. "Just an observation I've had while here, though—your spies among the student bodies tend to be Indian and Chinese foreign students."

A Warning from an Old Cop

Lenny let the words hang for a moment, his gaze steady. This kid was sharp, he'd give him that. Smart. Composed.

But Lenny didn't buy a word of it. "Coincidence that you're here? Don't believe that."

Lenny's voice was low, even. "But I'm not here to create an incident."

He leaned back slightly, still watching. "I'm retired. Old. Obviously, you know what I did in the RCMP. Your handler briefed you. And the RCMP know you're here. They're watching, same as me. The second they decide you're a problem; you'll be in cuffs."

Ethan remained unshaken; his face still unreadable.

Lenny let the silence stretch before adding, "But if I see you following me, or anywhere near my apartment—I'll do something about it."

Another pause.

"Ask your handler, if you don't already know, what sort of things I've done."

He held Ethan's gaze, waiting for a flicker of uncertainty.

Nothing.

Then, slowly, Ethan smiled. Relaxed. Almost amused. "Point taken," he said, nodding slightly. "Thank you."

Lenny stood, gave him one last look, then walked back to his friends.

He didn't look back. But he could feel those sharp blue eyes watching him all the same.

Made in Canada vs. Produced in Canada

That evening, he met Natalie to go over a new posting for TNSF:

> Made in Canada vs. Produced in Canada: What's the Difference?
>
> Understanding Product Labels
>
> Understanding product labels is essential when shopping for Canadian goods, but terms like "Made in Canada" and "Produced in Canada" can sometimes be confusing.
>
> Here's what they really mean:
>
> ✔ Made in Canada – A product labeled "Made in Canada" must have at least 51% of its total production costs (including materials, labor, and manufacturing) to be incurred in Canada.
>
> Additionally, the final transformation of the product must take place in Canada. Companies must also include a qualifier (e.g., "Made in Canada with imported ingredients").
>
> ✔ Produced in Canada – This term is often used

interchangeably with "Made in Canada," but it typically applies more to agricultural and food products.

It means that the product was primarily grown, raised, or processed in Canada, even if some ingredients were imported. Like "Made in Canada," a qualifier is required (e.g., "Produced in Canada from domestic and imported ingredients").

Why Does This Matter?

Understanding these labels helps consumers make informed decisions, whether they want to:

- Support local businesses
- Reduce their carbon footprint
- Ensure high-quality standards

Next time you shop, check the labels carefully and support Canadian-made and Canadian-produced products!

#MadeInCanada #ProducedInCanada #ShopLocal #SupportCanadianBusinesses

Lenny's Silence

That night, Lenny went to bed without telling Natalie about his meeting with Ethan Cole, CIA.

9

PAIN BEGINS TO REVEAL ITSELF

The Puppet Master

Travis Caldwell, Premier of Alberta, was wrapping up his high-stakes networking tour in Washington.

Over the past few days, he had spoken to:

- Senators.
- Representatives.
- Members of President Harland's cabinet.

At every turn, he pushed Alberta's interests.

This was his final meeting before boarding the Alberta government's private luxury jet. A meeting not with the elected leader of the free world—but with the man who truly pulled the strings.

That man was not President Harland. It was Grant Winthrop.

The Man Who Owned Power

A billionaire.

A genius in many regards.

A ghost in the world of power.

Winthrop operated in the shadows, a puppeteer whose influence shaped:

- Governments.
- Markets.
- Policies.

His vision for the world? Something out of Star Trek—a sleek, hyper-efficient civilization fuelled by unrelenting technological advancement.

And thanks to the hundreds of millions he had funnelled into Harland's election campaign, he had bought a president. A president who now granted him unfettered access to the federal budget, giving him the means to build his utopia.

The Real Agenda

But Winthrop's ambitions didn't stop at infrastructure and technology. He had another directive—Eliminate every trace of the Woke movement.

To the Harland administration, "Woke" was a political enemy, an ideological thorn in their side. Some argued it had gone too far, silencing dissent in the name of progress.

Winthrop? He didn't care about any of it. To him, dismantling Woke initiatives was just a favor to Harland. A way to maintain the illusion that he wasn't only advancing his own interests.

Because, in truth? Winthrop's real project was something far more radical. He wanted to restructure the world itself.

The Future Belongs to the Few

Winthrop didn't believe in democracy. Government by the people? Laughable. Government for the people? Even worse.

He often reminded those in his inner circle that America's founding fathers had originally restricted voting rights to white male landowners.

Even that, he believed, had been too generous. The world needed fewer decision-makers, not more. Only the brightest minds—minds like his—should hold the reins of power.

Harland? That fool?

Winthrop smirked to himself. He thinks he's in charge. If only he knew.

A Meeting with a Billionaire

When Caldwell entered Winthrop's office—a sleek, minimalist fortress just blocks from the White House—his eyes were drawn to the billionaire's expression: An artificial smile. A polite performance.

Then, he noticed Winthrop's gaze flick downward. Caldwell glanced at his own feet. The cowboy boots.

A hint of amusement crossed Winthrop's face. As if meeting with politicians—especially those from backwater places like Alberta—was merely an obligatory chore.

A Game of Power

Pleasantries were short. Winthrop mentioned spending part of his childhood in Saskatchewan, a fact Caldwell neither believed nor cared about.

The real conversation began the moment Caldwell leaned in. "Your brutal tariff on our cattle will increase your import costs by $1,100 per head."

His voice was sharp. "Your meat processors will pass that

straight to American consumers. Come July and August, your beloved BBQ season is going to be a disaster."

Winthrop's lips curled into a practiced, reassuring smile. A smile designed to feign sympathy.

But in reality? He didn't give a damn.

The Art of Manipulation

By mid-August, the complaints would peak. By September, they'd fade—drowned out by cooling weather and shifting political discourse.

People had short memories. That was the beauty of it.

Winthrop leaned back. "Look, Travis, I'll mention it to the President. You know I have his ear. But he's pretty set on this tariff."

Caldwell pressed on. "We've beefed up border security. Spent millions on new tech. Our Fentanyl Director is working directly with your federal team. We're securing the border."

Winthrop's expression didn't change. But his thoughts were loud. *I don't give a rat's ass about that. And neither does the President.*

Harland wasn't worried about security. He was obsessed with something much bigger—The prospect of Alberta itself. Rich with resources. Eventually folding into the United States.

Winthrop Ends the Meeting

Winthrop stood, signalling the meeting was over. He walked Caldwell to the door, his movements smooth, effortless.

The kind of confidence that came from knowing you held all the power. A handshake. An empty smile. A dismissal masked as courtesy.

As the door closed behind him, Winthrop returned to his desk, exhaling through his nose. *The world is already mine. They just don't know it yet.*

A Knock at the Door

A striking woman peeked inside. "Mr. Winthrop, the Arizona Governor and Mr. Galbraith are here for their appointment."

Winthrop barely looked up. "Shelley, in twenty minutes, I want you to knock and tell me I'm expected in the Attorney General's office."

She hesitated. "But sir... you don't—"

"Shelley, just do it. I don't want this meeting running over." With a nod, she retreated, closing the door behind her.

Another Crisis, Another Dismissal

Victor Galbraith launched into a frantic monologue about his hotel chain hemorrhaging money.

All because Canadians are canceling reservations.

The Arizona Governor, Rose Castro, took over, her voice tense. Thousands of Canadian Snowbirds are listing their homes and trailer park properties for sale. Their exodus threatens Arizona's housing market and, more importantly, the billions they inject into the state's winter economy.

Winthrop offered a practiced nod, but his mind was elsewhere. Blah, blah. Yada, yada. One ear in, the other out.

Right on cue, Shelley knocked. "Sir, the Attorney General is expecting you."

Perfect. He stood, extending a polite but firm smile. "Governor, Mr. Galbraith, I appreciate your time."

They shuffled out, their concerns unresolved, their urgency dismissed.

Finally, peace. Winthrop sunk back into his chair, fingers drumming against his desk.

That's the future. And if a few thousand bureaucrats lose their jobs? Well, that's just progress.

10

ONE OF THE MOLES

FBI Headquarters – Washington, D.C.

Special Agent Mark Grayson had spent seventeen years in the Bureau. He had joined the FBI to serve his country, to uphold the rule of law, to be a part of something bigger than himself.

Now, he barely recognized the institution he had once sworn to protect.

Director Dale Carver had been a brutal enforcer of Harland's vision. The once-proud Bureau had been gutted—loyalty tests, political purges, and mass layoffs had transformed it into a weapon of intimidation rather than justice.

Last week, Carver had gone a step further.

Thousands of career agents—people who had spent their lives fighting organized crime, terrorism, and corruption—were suddenly terminated. No hearings, no due process. Just an unceremonious email and an escort out the door.

That was bad enough.

But what really enraged Grayson—what made him break his own rules—was that Carver had deliberately released the names and personal details of every agent deemed "disloyal."

These were people with families, people who had spent decades going after the worst criminals America had to offer. And now, thanks to Carver's stunt, every cartel, every extremist cell, every foreign intelligence agency that had ever been under FBI surveillance had access to home addresses, family members, and retirement locations.

Harland had painted targets on their backs.

Grayson clenched his fists. It wasn't just an act of political retaliation. It was a death sentence for those agents. And Carver knew it.

The Bureau wasn't about the law anymore. It was about fear. And Grayson had reached his limit.

Encrypted Chat – The Whistleblower and Perez

He had to move fast.

Alone in a dimly lit back office, he powered up a secure terminal on his burner laptop. He didn't have long. The IT team had been getting too good at tracking unauthorized logins.

He logged into the encrypted channel. His contact was waiting.

> Grayson: You need to act now. I have something major.

> Raul Perez (PDM): What happened?

> Grayson: It's worse than we thought. The purges? They weren't just firings. The Bureau released the personal information of every agent deemed 'disloyal.' Names, home addresses, family details. These people are being hunted.

> Perez: Jesus Christ.

> Grayson: And there's more. Something bigger. Winthrop has breached the government payment system. His companies are now processing federal transactions. He has direct access to every financial transaction made by the U.S. government.

> Perez: That's unconstitutional.

> Grayson: It's treason. Harland handed him the keys, and no one is stopping him. You need to file legal action NOW.

> Perez: We'll get the best lawyers on it. But we need proof.

Grayson hesitated; his fingers poised over the keyboard.

> Grayson: I can get you the documents. But if I'm caught, I'm finished.

> Perez: Then don't take the risk. Get out.

Grayson exhaled.

> Grayson: Too late for that.

And he logged out.

FBI Director's Office – Moments Later

Grayson moved quickly. He wiped his logs, shut down the laptop, and prepared to walk out as if nothing had happened. But the moment he turned, a voice stopped him cold. "What the hell are you doing in here, Grayson?"

His breath caught.

Director Dale Carver stood in the doorway, his arms folded, his sharp eyes scanning the darkened room.

For a moment, neither man spoke.

Grayson forced a calm expression. "Sir. Just finishing up casework."

Carver stepped forward. His bulk blocked the exit.

"That's not your workstation," Carver said flatly. "And I don't recall assigning you to anything involving secure logins."

Grayson's pulse thundered. Stay calm. Stay in control.

"Had to check a flagged suspect," he lied. "Cyber division asked me to confirm something."

Carver's gaze flicked to the laptop.

And he smiled. It wasn't friendly. "Step away from the desk."

Grayson hesitated.

Carver's voice dropped. "Now."

Slowly, Grayson moved back as Carver circled the desk. He flipped open the laptop. His fingers moved across the keys, searching.

A long silence.

Then Carver's smirk widened. "You know, Mark," he said casually, "I was just about to run an internal audit on unauthorized data access."

Grayson kept his face neutral. "Sir, I don't know what you're implying—"

Carver held up a hand. "Save it."

He exhaled through his nose, shaking his head like a disappointed father. "You're a smart guy. You've lasted this long without making a move. But I knew one of you was leaking information." He tapped the laptop screen. "And here you are."

Grayson didn't move. Didn't speak.

"You know what's funny?" Carver mused. "You could've just quit. Walked away. But no—you had to be a hero."

He turned, stepping dangerously close. "Do you think the PDM will save you?" he murmured. "They won't. Harland won't even have to lift a finger. You'll disappear, and no one will even ask where you went."

Grayson met his gaze, refusing to blink.

Carver studied him for a moment. Then he sighed. "I need you to come with me."

Grayson's stomach dropped. "Where to?" he asked evenly.

Carver's smirk returned. "The interrogation wing."

The Race Against Time

As Grayson was escorted down the hall, Perez was already in motion.

The Pro-Democracy Movement activated its emergency protocol. If the FBI was preparing for a crackdown, they had to act first.

Perez reached out to his legal contacts. The case had to be filed within 24 hours. If Winthrop controlled the government's payment system, he controlled everything—funding for states, for military operations, for critical agencies.

This was bigger than they had imagined. Grayson had bought them time, but if they failed? By morning, the Pro-Democracy Movement would be crippled.

And Grayson? He wouldn't be coming home.

11

THE BELLIGERENT

The Gathering of the Discarded

The church hall in a quiet Washington suburb was packed. A hundred former federal employees had gathered, their voices hushed, but their frustrations palpable.

These were not ordinary workers—They were seasoned public servants:

- Former FBI agents.
- Justice Department prosecutors.
- International aid administrators.
- Inspectors general.

Dismissed en masse in the early weeks of President Harland's second term, they had spent their careers upholding the institutions of democracy, only to find themselves discarded.

Winthrop's Retaliation

They were here to discuss:

- Their futures.
- Severance.
- Retirement benefits.
- The looming threat of legal entanglements.

Garth Winthrop—now the most powerful unelected figure in America, had made it clear: he intended to slash their entitlements. And where possible, he would paint their dismissals as terminations for cause.

Those who had:

- Pursued investigations against Harland.
- Resisted his administration.
- Once wielded power in service of the Constitution.

Winthrop was determined to strip them of protection and brand them as enemies.

Fired, but Not Defeated

Yet, despite their predicament, there was a steely resolve in the room.

These were men and women who had served under both Republican and Democratic administrations—without bias.

They had:

- Defended America against terrorism, lawlessness, economic collapse, and pandemics.
- Fought for justice when it was inconvenient.
- Protected institutions that were now being dismantled.

They had been fired, but they were not dead.

The motto passed in whispers from table to table: "Fired, but not dead."

The Pro-Democracy Movement (PDM)

Among the attendees were:

- Key figures from the Pro-Democracy Movement (PDM).
- Disillusioned politicians.
- Activists.
- Former public servants.

They had spent the last four years fighting the rightward shift of the Republican Party.

They had poured millions into attack ads against Harland. They had fought against his allies during the election. And they had failed.

Now? They sought to regroup. And for that? They needed:

- The expertise of these former officials.
- Their knowledge.
- Their voices.

Because what they feared most was becoming reality. A creeping authoritarianism.

The Warning

In one corner of the hall, a small group gathered.

- Raul Perez – A former Attorney General from a Republican administration two decades prior.
- A former FBI senior agent.
- An ex-prosecutor from the Justice Department.

Perez, known for his sharp intellect and historical perspective, leaned in. "This is how it begins."

His voice was low, grave.

"We've seen it before. Germany. The 1930s. The slow march to authoritarianism."

Denying the Inevitable

The prosecutor shook his head.

"Come on, Raul. The situations aren't remotely comparable.Germany was crippled by war debt, politically unstable, and had no history of real democracy. America has 250 years of constitutional governance, a Supreme Court, checks and balances."

Perez exhaled sharply. "You're assuming those checks still work. Are they independent?"

He tapped his finger on the table. "The Court just ruled that a president can't be held responsible for his actions while governing."

"They rolled back fundamental rights women have had for decades—exactly what the far right has been pushing for."

"And Congress?" He let out a mirthless chuckle.

"Harland calls, and the Republican senators and representatives fall in line." "Their loyalty isn't to the Constitution. It's to him."

Who Holds the Real Power?

The former FBI agent folded his arms. "And Winthrop?"

Perez nodded grimly. "That's the real question, isn't it? Who holds the power—The president or the oligarch who controls the economy?"

The prosecutor frowned. "State governors are still a check on federal overreach."

Perez's voice dropped to a whisper. "And how many are Republican?"

Silence.

The Papers That Changed Everything

Perez reached into his briefcase. Pulled out a stack of papers. Spread them across the table—Documents. News reports. Financial records.

"This is what we should be afraid of."

The former FBI agent's eyes narrowed. "What am I looking at?"

Perez tapped a page in the centre. "Winthrop's team has secured access to the Treasury Department's payment infrastructure."

The FBI agent's jaw clenched. "Meaning?"

Perez's tone was grim. "That's five trillion dollars in government disbursements—Social Security, federal salaries, pensions. He controls it now."

The Data That Made Them Targets

Perez flipped to another page. "And it's not just that. They've gained access to sensitive data—federal employees' personal records, contractor details."

He looked up. "They know who worked against them. They know where they live. Their families. Their finances."

The prosecutor flipped through the pages. His expression darkened. "How did this happen? Who signed off on this?"

Perez's mouth twisted into something like a smile—but there was no humour in it. "No one had to sign off. That's the point."

He tapped his finger on the final page—A summary of Winthrop's recent acquisitions and political moves.

Winthrop's Power Play

1. Financial Power:

- Banks had just sold off $5.5 billion in debt tied to Winthrop's financial empire—a sign that investors had absolute faith in him.

The Realization

The former FBI agent exhaled. "Jesus Christ."

Perez nodded slowly. "Exactly."

Winthrop's Grip Tightens

Perez tapped the final pages of the stack. "And here's why we should be afraid." He slid them across the table, his finger hovering over key points.

2. Corporate Influence

- Visa.
- United Airlines.
- Amazon.

Winthrop's companies were entering deep financial and operational partnerships with some of the biggest corporations in the country. They weren't just clients . They were becoming his extensions. Control the corporations, control the economy.

3. Political Control

"It's not just money. It's power. His influence extended beyond economic dominance. The White House had quietly granted him advisory control over: Federal workforce restructuring.

Which meant? Winthrop had the ability to purge career officials, all <u>under</u> the guise of efficiency. FBI agents, prosecutors, intelligence officials, scientists—Anyone inconvenient could be erased.

And no one would call it political. They'd call it 'modernization.'

4. Unprecedented Wealth

"His net worth just crossed $400 billion."

Perez's voice was almost disbelieving. "The first human in history to reach that milestone."

And he wasn't stopping. He wasn't just rich. He was untouchable.

The Question No One Wanted to Answer

Perez looked up at his companions. His expression darkened. "Tell me, gentlemen—who really runs this country?"

Silence.

The murmurs in the room seemed to grow louder—Conversations. Alliances. Strategies forming.

The Fight Wasn't Over.

Not yet.

12

BLUE RODEO CONCERT

A Night of Music

Lenny hummed *Lost Together* under his breath as he and Natalie stepped out of the concert hall, the echoes of Blue Rodeo's performance still vibrating in the air.

He was in high spirits—His favourite band. One of his dearest friends.

Listening to Blue Rodeo together had become their tradition. Whether at his place or hers. Sharing a drink. Unwinding.

A Familiar Face in the Crowd

Natalie smiled; her eyes bright. "That was wonderful—absolutely wonderful. They played for two hours."

Lenny nodded, still lost in the afterglow of the show.

But then—just as suddenly, his mood darkened. His jaw tightened. His stomach twisted. "You Son of a Bitch."

There. In the crowded lobby, among the other concertgoers, stood Ethan Cole. Lenny barely hesitated. "Excuse me, Natalie," he said, already moving toward Cole.

The Confrontation

Cole, beer in hand, barely had time to register the sudden presence before Lenny was upon him. He flinched, startled—But just for a second. Then his cool exterior returned. "Great show, Lenny, don't you think?" Cole took a casual sip of his drink.

Lenny's voice was low, dangerous. "I told you not to follow me."

Cole smirked. "You're being paranoid, Lenny. It's a free country. I happen to love Blue Rodeo."

Natalie's Connection to Cole

Before Lenny could respond, Natalie appeared beside them. To his surprise, she greeted Cole with familiarity. "Well, hello, Ethan."

Lenny's head snapped toward her. What the hell?

Cole's smirk widened. "Professor Cheng. What a pleasant surprise. Are you here with Lenny?"

Natalie nodded. "Yes." Then she turned to Lenny, curious. "Wait… you two know each other?"

Cole didn't miss a beat. "We met a while back. Just briefly."

His tone was almost playful. Then he added—"Lenny's a bit of a legend, you know."

Lenny's Past—Unspoken

Lenny's blood ran cold. His hands clenched into fists.

"Don't." His voice was strained with warning.

Natalie laughed. "Oh, I wouldn't call him a legend. He's a spokesperson in Saskatchewan, promoting Canadian sovereignty. He's a good writer, sure. But a legend?"

She chuckled. "That's a stretch."

Cole's grin sharpened. "Oh… you don't know about his police background?"

Lenny's fingernails dug into his palms.

Cole's Exit

Cole winked. "I gotta go. Nice seeing you, Professor. You too, Lenny."

He turned. Walked to the bar. Placed his half-finished beer on the counter, and strode out the door.

Lenny's Realization

Lenny exhaled sharply, turning to Natalie. "How do you know him?"

Natalie shrugged. "Oh, he's in one of my classes. Bright, enthusiastic student."

Lenny narrowed his eyes.

Coincidence? A student in her class. A fan of Blue Rodeo.

Here tonight, of all places. That young man made him nervous.

Natalie's Story

A Quiet Night In

They sat in Natalie's small living room, nestled in her modest one-bedroom apartment.

The space was sparsely furnished—

- A short chesterfield.
- A single armchair.
- A coffee table stacked with books on economic theory.

A room of intellect, not comfort. A reflection of Natalie herself.

A Late-Night Conversation

Lenny occupied the chesterfield. Natalie curled up in the armchair, a glass of Pinot Grigio in hand.

Lenny nursed a beer. His fourth.

He glanced at her. "Natalie, you've never really told me much about yourself."

She smirked, swirling her wine. "I grew up in Regina. Went to school here until I started my doctorate at Queen's."

Lenny leaned forward. "Come on, more than that. What did your parents do? Siblings? And there's got to be some juicy love story in there."

She let out a small laugh.

The wine loosened her usual restraint.

Natalie's Past

"I grew up in Whitmore Park, just a mile from here. My older brother is a cardiac specialist in Calgary."

Her smile softened. "My parents were teachers—wonderful people.

They'd be your age if they were still alive."

Her voice dipped slightly. "My mother died of cancer. My father followed not long after. Broken heart, they say."

She took a slow sip—Swallowing down the grief that never fully left.

Then, with a playful grin, she added—"I loved a boy when I was twelve, but that didn't work out. Too painful. So, I figured, why bother trying again?"

She laughed lightly, but there was an edge of truth beneath the humour.

"And anyway, I love my work. The university world keeps me surrounded by like-minded people. That's enough for me."

The Legend Speaks

She turned the conversation back on him. Her eyes sharp. "Now, Lenny the Legend—spill. Give me something because my curiosity isn't going anywhere."

The Past, Unspoken

Lenny hesitated. He never shared. Too many regrets. Too many things he wished he could undo.

Would she think less of him? That was always the fear.

A Truth Long Buried

But the beers had loosened his tongue.

And somehow—He felt safe here. With her.

He sighed, then spoke. "Natalie, I have a checkered past."

His voice was quieter now. "I joined the RCMP at twenty-three, right after university. Trained at Depot here in Regina."

A pause.

"That's where I met Valerie." A faint smile ghosted his lips.

"She was a local girl. We got married, believing in 'til death do us part.' But it wasn't a good deal for her."

The RCMP Years

Lenny exhaled, staring into his beer. "My first posting was in a small town in northern British Columbia. Isolated. Hard life.

"Valerie was expected to help with the Force activities—unpaid, of course. We had two boys. Then I got transferred to Vancouver."

His jaw tightened. "Valerie was ecstatic—finally, a real city.

No more nomadic living. But Vancouver was where everything changed."

Undercover Shadows

"I started working undercover."

Lenny's voice dropped lower. "I was away all the time. I couldn't talk to her about my work. Couldn't share anything. My boys grew up without me."

A bitter smile flickered across his lips. "And the deeper I went, the darker I became. I crossed lines. A lot of them."

Lines That Couldn't Be Uncrossed

Lenny set his beer down, staring at the label as if searching for redemption in its condensation. "I don't like talking about it, but I did things, Natalie.

"I let criminals think their own kind had betrayed them—knowing it would get them killed."

"I beat a man to death to protect my cover."

"I became someone else entirely."

A long silence.

"But I helped crack some of the biggest cases in Western Canada. When I finally left the field, I spent two years training the next generation of undercover officers at Depot. That was my last job before retirement."

The Cost of His Choices

Lenny glanced at her, gauging her reaction. "My wife—Valerie—she's gone now. Cancer took her."

His voice faltered. "I had retired by then. We thought we'd finally have time together."

A long breath. "We didn't."

He looked away. "My boys—well, they call me sometimes. Out of obligation, I think. I wasn't really a father to them. I was just... absent."

A heavy silence settled between them.

The Legend, Unmasked

Lenny leaned back, running a hand over his face. "So, there you go, Natalie."

His voice was quieter now. "That's me. The legend you were so curious about."

The Weight of Leadership

But no response came—only a long silence.

Natalie finally spoke. "How are you holding up, Lenny?

You know, with your involvement in TNSF?"

Lenny sighed, running a hand through his hair. He didn't sugarcoat it. "I'm mentally and physically exhausted."

Natalie studied him. "You look it, Lenny."

A Life Once Simpler

Lenny exhaled, shaking his head. "I liked what I was doing before."

His voice was tinged with nostalgia. "Digging through old newspapers. Uncovering forgotten true crime stories. Turning them into books—whether fact or fiction."

He glanced at her. "My sales covered my publishing costs, and that was enough."

A small shrug. "But now?"

He shook his head, frustration creeping in.

"You folks write for me. Slap my name on it. Send me out to talk to crowds.

"And when I do? I feel like Walter Matthau trying to play a romantic lead."

His grin was bitter. "Who the hell would want to kiss that face? Who the hell would want to follow my advice?"

The Impact, Real and Measurable

Natalie winced. "Geez, Lenny. I hate seeing you like this."

"But for what it's worth? You and your counterparts in other provinces are making an incredible impact."

She pulled out her phone, scrolled, then read aloud:

A Nation Reacts

"Bye, America. We canceled our family vacation to Oceanside, Oregon, the same day the proposed tariffs were announced. That's four families—fourteen people—who would have spent seven days in the U.S. Accommodation, food, gas, activities, restaurants—$15K to $20K CAD, gone."

"We're not anti-American, but these tariffs on Canadian goods make no sense. If they go through after the 30-day pause, they'll devastate our economy. So, we pivoted—we're going to Whistler instead."

The Reality of His Success

Lenny exhaled sharply. "Yeah."

A pause. "My books are selling like never before."

A rueful chuckle. "I'm raking in money. More than I ever expected."

He leaned back. "And I've been donating it to TNSF."

A shrug. "So, I guess it ain't all bad."

Natalie's Concern

Natalie gave him a long, searching look. "Lenny, I want you to see a doctor."

Lenny chuckled, shaking his head. "Sure, Natalie. I need a check-up anyway."

But in his mind? He already knew. The tests were full of bad news.

13

THE TARIFF TRAGEDY

Southern Saskatchewan – A Hot Summer Night

Dale slammed the case of beer onto the old wooden table on his back porch. The sun dipped below the wheat fields, casting long shadows across his yard. The smell of burnt burgers hung in the air.

The Toast of Bitterness

Rick cracked open a can. "Well, boys, here's to another damn year of working twice as hard for half as much."

Marty snorted. "If that."

They all clinked cans and took long gulps.

The Tariff Stranglehold

For months now, the tariffs had been choking the life out of their livelihoods.

First, the Americans slapped a 25% tariff on:

- Grain.
- Steel.

Then Ottawa struck back with its own. Prices skyrocketed. Sales dried up.

What little money they had? Straight to the banks and credit unions. Or into the ground—hoping the next crop would save them.

A Future Unraveling

Dale leaned back; his face red—not just from the beer, but from anger that had been brewing for months. "I had a buyer down in Montana. Big contract. Would've cleared my debts."

A pause. "Then—bam! Tariffs hit, deal's off. Now I'm drowning in grain no one wants."

Rick nodded, wiping sweat from his forehead. "My feed costs are through the roof. No one in the States is buying my beef. I had to cull half my herd last month."

A pained expression crossed his face. "Never thought I'd have to put down healthy animals. Just 'cause I couldn't afford to keep 'em."

Tensions Rise

Marty swirled his beer, "You should've diversified before this all hit, Dale. You too, Rick. Can't rely on one thing anymore."

Dale's eyes darkened. "Oh, so it's our fault, is it?"

Rick scoffed. "Marty, your damn shop is barely keeping its doors open. Last I checked, nobody's got the money to hire a welder when they're losing their land."

Marty rolled his eyes. "I planned for this. I saw it coming. You two just sat on your asses thinking things would stay the same forever."

Dale's can slammed down so hard that beer sloshed onto the table. "You smug son of a—"

Marty shot up from his chair. "What? What are you gonna do? Blame Ottawa? Blame Washington? Maybe blame the Chinese while you're at it?"

A Fist, A Fall

Dale's face twisted. He had just enough beer in him to let his rage take control. "You're standing there acting like you're some goddamn business genius, when you're just as screwed as the rest of us!"

Marty smirked. "Least I'm not crying into my beer about it."

And that was it. That was the moment. The last thing Marty saw before it all went black was Dale's fist coming straight at his jaw.

The Fight

The metal lawn chair toppled over. A beer can burst open, spraying foam across the dirt.

Marty hit the ground, but he was on his feet in a second. He swung—a beer bottle in his hand. Glass shattered against Dale's shoulder.

Rick jumped in, shoving them apart. "Jesus Christ! What the hell is wrong with you two?!"

The Breaking Point

Dale, breathing hard, turned back to Marty. "You think you're better than us?!"

Marty, blood running from his lip, laughed. "I know I am."

And that was the last thing he ever said.

A Wrench, A Fatal Blow

Dale grabbed the first thing he could find—a heavy wrench from the BBQ table. And swung.

A sickening crack rang through the yard. Marty collapsed.

The Weight of Realization

Rick froze. His breath hitched. "Marty?"

No response.

"Marty!"

Rick dropped to his knees. He shook Marty. Checked for his pulse. His hands trembled. His face turned pale.

"Oh, God. Oh, no, no, no—"

Dale stood there, the wrench still in his hand. His face drained of all colour. "I didn't mean to—"

Rick fumbled for his phone. "Jesus Christ, Dale, he's not breathing!"

The Arrival of the RCMP

The flashing red-and-blues lit up the night. The silence was broken only by:

- The chirp of the radio.
- The sound of boots crunching across dry grass.

Two RCMP officers stepped into the yard.

The younger one, Constable Hayes, moved quickly to check Marty.

But the older officer? Sergeant Bishop already knew the truth. He let out a slow breath, rubbing a hand down his face. "This is happening throughout the province far too often."

A Province Unraveling

Rick sat on the steps, head in his hands, shaking.

Dale stood motionless, his eyes glassy, his hands stained with something darker than grease.

Hayes shook his head. "Another farm town, another backyard fight that went too far."

The Arrest

Bishop looked at Dale. "Turn around."

Dale did as he was told. The cold snap of the cuffs echoed through the night. As Bishop led Dale toward the cruiser, the old farmer finally choked out—"I didn't mean to… I didn't mean to…"

Bishop didn't even look at him. "None of you ever do."

Several Days Later – Regina, Saskatchewan

Sergeant Randy Bishop drove to Regina, a simple errand—

Princess Auto. It had been months since he last saw his father. So, he decided to stop by.

There was still time. Maybe grab a bite to eat at Montana's.

He called ahead.

The Call

"Dad, it's Randy."

Lenny's voice came through, steady and familiar. "Hey, what's up?"

Randy hesitated, then asked, "Feel like grabbing dinner at Montana's?"

A beat of silence. Then—"Sure, but I'm buying."

Normally, they'd argue over that.

But tonight? Randy let it go. He didn't want old wounds reopened. Didn't want another round of his father's attempts to make amends.

Tonight, he just wanted—To show Lenny pictures of his kids. To talk about life. To keep things simple.

The Meeting at Montana's

Montana's wasn't busy. They found a table right away.

Randy pulled out his phone, scrolling through photos of his four kids, aged four to thirteen.

Lenny studied them, eyes soft. "Geez, Randy, I'm proud of you. You're so much—"

A pause.

Randy cut in, shaking his head. "Stop, Dad. The past is the past. No need to go there."

Lenny exhaled, giving a small nod. "Alright."

A beat. Then—"Have you heard from Reggie lately?"

Reggie – The Youngest

Randy sighed, setting down his drink. "No, but I heard he might be out of work."

Lenny leaned back, rubbing his chin. "He was with Brandt Industries. They laid off a lot of people."

His jaw tightened. "If I had to guess? He's hitting the booze hard. That's what he does when things fall apart."

A pause. "I should reach out to him. I really should."

Randy took a sip, voice neutral. "He actually called me last week."

Lenny looked up.

"Wanted to stay with us for a while." Randy shook his head. His latest girlfriend threw him out. Same reason as always."

A long sigh. "I told him we just don't have the space."

Then, carefully—"But maybe he could crash on your chesterfield for a few nights? You could help him get back on his feet."

Lenny rubbed his temple, then nodded. "Yeah... yeah, I'll do that."

He pulled out his phone, sliding it across the table. "Type in his number for me."

Randy did, knowing full well—Reggie was as unsettled as ever.

Talk of Work & Division

After a pause, Lenny shifted gears. "So... do you mind me asking about work?"

Randy hesitated, then shrugged. "Dad, you must've heard about the BBQ death?"

Lenny nodded. "Yeah."

Randy exhaled. "Tensions are high. People are scared."

He shook his head. "Small manufacturers can't sell south of the border. Businesses are shutting down."

A beat. "But honestly? That's not the real problem."

Lenny lifted his eyes to meet his son's, searching for traces of his wife's influence—the qualities she had instilled that he hadn't. A caring father, a devoted husband, a respected leader—everything Lenny had wished to be but couldn't, not while living undercover.

"Dad, are you listening?"

Lenny blinked, pulled from his thoughts. "Ah, yes, Randy. Go ahead."

"The real issue is the locals who supported President Harland before he was elected. They're suffering from the tariffs but would rather blame our government. The pre-election tension between them and those who despise Harland has only escalated."

As they talked, Lenny found himself studying his son with admiration, while Randy spoke passionately about his work.

14

DIALOGUE

Mid-Summer Evening – Virtual Meeting

Ottawa & Washington

The tension crackled like a live wire as the virtual meeting commenced.

In Washington, President Jefferson Harland sat rigidly behind the Resolute Desk, his expression carved in stone.

To his right, Chief of Staff Margaret Kellerman.

To his left, billionaire Garth Winthrop, his most influential financial backer.

They flanked him like sentinels.

In Ottawa, Prime Minister Geneviève Lacroix sat calmly, quiet confidence radiating from her.

Beside her, Chief of Staff Robin Hay. Ready. Watching. Calculating.

The Game is Bigger Than Tariffs

This wasn't just a trade negotiation—It was a battle of survival.

Harland had no intention of lowering tariffs. He wanted to crush Canada's economy, break its political will, and force annexation in the long game.

His administration had systematically crippled Canadian industries by imposing:

- Crippling 25% tariffs on key sectors.
- Economic warfare designed to drive Lacroix's approval ratings into the ground.

The plan? Keep the pressure up. Force Canada to buckle. Make them come crawling to the U.S.—on his terms.

But now? Things weren't going as planned.

The Unexpected Backfire

The European Union was courting Canada for a freer trade deal, sensing weakness in the American market.

Canada's removal of interprovincial trade barriers had:

✓ Strengthened its economy.

✓ Created new market opportunities.

✓ United the provinces against U.S. aggression.

And worst of all? The U.S. fruit and vegetable growers—especially in Florida, Texas, and Arizona—were suffering. Red States. Harland's voter base.

✓ Florida's citrus industry was collapsing.

✓ Texas beef exports were drying up.

✓ Arizona was bleeding as Snowbirds pulled their money out.

And Canada's retirees? They were already moving their wealth elsewhere.

The Negotiation

Harland exhaled sharply, his frustration barely contained. "Alright, let's get this over with. We're keeping tariffs at twenty-five percent. That's final."

Lacroix didn't flinch. She folded her hands neatly on the table, tilting her head slightly. "You're mistaken, Mr. President."

Harland's eyes narrowed. "Excuse me?"

Lacroix's voice was steady, firm. "You're not keeping them at twenty-five percent."

Silence.

The Power Shift

Harland's knuckles turned white against the desk. "The hell we aren't."

Lacroix remained composed. "Your country is hemorrhaging. U.S. farmers are drowning because of our retaliatory tariffs."

She paused, letting the words sink in. "Florida's citrus industry? Collapsing. Texas beef? Export market drying up. Arizona? Snowbirds pulling out. Losing billions."

Her voice remained smooth, deliberate. "And let's not forget, Mr. President—Arizona, Florida, and Texas? They're all red states. They voted for you. And right now? They're feeling the pain."

Harland's face darkened, but Kellerman pressed a warning hand against his arm, urging restraint.

Lacroix leaned forward; eyes locked onto Harland's. "Do you know who isn't feeling the pain? Canada."

Canada's Resilience

Robin Hay slid a report toward the camera.

"Since removing interprovincial trade barriers, our economy

has stabilized. Unemployment is dropping. The European Union is aggressively pursuing a trade deal with us."

Harland's pulse thundered. "Bullshit," he snarled.

Lacroix allowed herself the smallest smile. "Oh, it's very real.

"While you were busy trying to choke us out, we adapted. You thought Canada would crawl back, begging for relief. Instead, we've made deals that make your tariffs obsolete."

A pause. "And the moment we sign with the EU? Your leverage over us is gone."

Kellerman's jaw tightened. She knew it was true.

Harland shifted in his chair, frustration mounting. "Your poll numbers are in the damn toilet, Lacroix. You need this more than I do."

Lacroix shrugged, unaffected. "And yet, here we are."

Her voice was calm, unwavering. "You? Sitting in Washington. Forced to negotiate with me."

A pause. Then, with measured confidence—"And your poll numbers?

Not so great either."

She gestured toward the screen. "Your annual inflation is 6.1%. Your tariffs on China are bleeding your economy. Americans are consumers, and they hate inflation."

Harland felt the walls closing in.

Winthrop Sees the Shift

Winthrop, always a step ahead, muttered something into Harland's ear, his voice low. Urgent. Calculating.

Harland hated this. He needed to keep Canada weak. A desperate Canada? An easy Canada.

The long game was simple—Force Canada's economy into submission. Make annexation the only way out.

But now? He was the one bleeding. And Lacroix knew it.

A Shift in Power. A New Reality.

For the first time since this war began—Harland wasn't dictating the terms.

Harland's Fury – The Oval Office

The moment the screen went black, Jefferson Harland erupted. "That insufferable bitch!" The coffee cup shattered, porcelain exploding against the wall.

Kellerman remained still, hands folded. Watching. Calculating.

Winthrop leaned against the desk, unbothered. Amused, even.

"She fucking humiliated me," Harland seethed, pacing like a caged animal. "She forced my hand! Me! The President of the goddamn United States!"

Winthrop exhaled, adjusting his cufflinks. "You had no choice, Jeff. You would've lost your own states."

Harland spun on him, eyes blazing. "I don't care about my fucking states! I care about Canada knowing it just won."

His breath came sharp, furious. "And if Canada thinks it can win? It won't stop. They'll keep pushing back. Keep aligning with the EU. Keep growing stronger until we lose our chance to break them."

Harland turned to Kellerman, breathing hard. "We were supposed to starve them out, Margaret. Make them desperate. Make them need us."

A pause. "And now?"

His eyes darkened. "Now they're emboldened."

Silence stretched.

Kellerman remained unreadable.

Harland's rage turned into something darker.

A New Strategy

His fists clenched. His vision swam with fury.

But there was no way out. If he refused to lower tariffs—his own states would revolt. His financial backers would turn on him. He had lost.

And she knew it.

The Order

"Get the FBI Director in here. Now."

Kellerman stiffened. "Jeff, let's think this through—"

Harland's voice cut through the room like a blade. "Now."

A tense silence gripped the office. The aide bolted out the door,

Moments later—FBI Director Dale Carver entered. "Mr. President."

Harland's gaze locked onto him. Cold. Calculating. Steel. "Dale, what would it take to push Canada further?"

Carver's eyes flicked between Kellerman and Winthrop, measuring the air.

A brief pause. Then—"A border incident, sir."

Kellerman's stomach knotted. She had feared Harland might spiral—But this? This was beyond reckless. This was dangerous.

Silence stretched.

Harland's lips curled into a thin smirk. The long game had shifted. Harland wasn't just waging economic war anymore.

The Prime Minister's Office – Ottawa

The air was heavy, not with victory. With tension.

Prime Minister Geneviève Lacroix sat at the edge of her desk, arms folded, watching the storm clouds gather over the Ottawa skyline.

Across from her, Chief of Staff Robin Hay exhaled sharply. "That was close."

Lacroix turned; eyes sharp. "No, Robin. That was a battle. The war is still on."

Strategic Patience

She straightened, gesturing toward him, I want a news release drafted. But it goes out only after the Americans report it first."

Robin frowned. "If we announce first, Harland will sabotage it."

Lacroix nodded. "He's not a man who lets his losses stand."

Robin hesitated, then sighed. "Not that I disagree, but... do you really think Harland would go that far? The deal is done."

Lacroix scoffed. "A deal is never done with Jefferson Harland."

She turned, pacing toward the window. "He's a man without ideology, without limits."

A pause. "His only principle is power."

The Real Threat

Robin sighed, rubbing his temples. "That makes him even more dangerous."

Lacroix nodded slowly. "Yes. It does."

A long silence. Robin finally spoke. "I still can't believe how badly he wanted to keep the tariffs in place. His own states were bleeding."

Lacroix glanced over her shoulder. "Because tariffs were never the goal. Breaking us was."

Robin frowned. "And after that?"

A beat. Then, Lacroix's voice dropped. "Annexation."

Robin exhaled sharply. "Jesus."

Lacroix continued. "You've seen the reports. California's wildfires—worse every year. Arable land shrinking. Water shortages spreading. The West and Southwest are running out of options."

Robin's lips tightened. "And we have the biggest freshwater supply in the world."

Lacroix nodded. "Harland doesn't just want our economy weak. He wants us desperate so that when the crisis in the U.S. spirals out of control—Canada is too broken to resist whatever he has planned."

Robin stared at the floor. "It's starting to feel like the 1930s all over again."

Lacroix raised an eyebrow.

Robin's voice grew somber. "Harland's vision is painfully clear. He wants expansion. Lebensraum—land and resources. Just like Germany before the war."

A pause.

Robin continued. "He doesn't want to 'work with' Canada. He wants to absorb us."

Lacroix inhaled slowly, nodding. "That's why we can't afford to relax. The ten percent tariff reduction is a short-term win. Nothing more. We're only safe when his government is gone."

A Drink Before the Next Battle

She turned, opening a cabinet behind her desk to remove a bottle of red wine. She uncorked it smoothly, pouring two glasses.

Robin raised an eyebrow. "Celebration?"

Lacroix handed him a glass. "Not at all.l. The fight isn't over. After what we just faced, we need to release some tension."

Robin clinked his glass against hers. "To endurance, then."

Lacroix gave a faint smile. "To endurance."

As they drank, the weight of what had just happened settled over them.

This wasn't over. Not by a long shot.

15

THE RED RIVER BORDER SKIRMISH

Southern Manitoba – A Cold Evening

The late afternoon sun hung low, casting long shadows over the snow-dusted fields. An icy wind swept across the prairie, rustling the dry grass along the dirt road.

Two vehicles idled. Two groups faced off.

And in the middle of nowhere, a plan was about to unfold.

The Meeting

The four Americans had crossed into Canada at Emerson just hours earlier. Their arrival was unremarkable. Their intentions were anything but.

The Canadian contacts—local sympathizers—stood waiting in a dark pickup, their breath visible in the crisp winter air. Without a word, they handed over the weapons.

Cole Danner, the American leader, inspected a semi-automatic rifle, feeling the cold steel.

One of the Canadians shifted nervously. "You sure about this?"

Danner smirked, loading a magazine. "Just stick to the plan. We'll handle the rest."

The groups parted ways.

The Canadians vanished into the night.

The Americans pressed forward—toward Highway 75. Toward the border. Toward the waiting trucks. Toward chaos.

The Blockade

The convoy of long-haul trucks rumbled toward the U.S. border, their headlights piercing the darkness.

Then—

Screech! A black SUV swerved sideways, blocking the highway. Brakes slammed. Horns blared.

Then—

Armed men spilled onto the road. Rifles were raised. Commands were shouted. "Step out! Hands where we can see them!"

The lead trucker hesitated. "You can't be serious."

"Serious as a heart attack," one shooter growled.

One by one, the truckers climbed down, hands raised.

The militia climbed onto trailers, ripping tarps aside, yanking containers open. Searching. Drugs? Weapons?

No. This wasn't about stopping fentanyl. This was about igniting a fire.

RCMP Responds

At the Emerson RCMP Detachment, the radio call came in hot. "Armed blockade. Highway 75."

The Staff Sergeant scowled. "Patch me through to Manitoba Command. Mobilize the Emergency Response Team. Now."

Within minutes, RCMP tactical units hit the road. Armoured vehicles roared south. Lights flashing. Sirens screaming.

Inside the lead vehicle, Sergeant Alex Ward checked his rifle. He turned to his team. "Negotiators go first. If they don't back down—We end it."

The Standoff

The blue and red lights painted the night.

RCMP SUVs boxed the blockade in. There was no escape.

A negotiator stepped forward; hands raised. "You're heavily armed on Canadian soil. This ends now."

Danner smirked. "We're doing your job, officer. Keeping fentanyl off U.S. streets. You should be thanking us."

The negotiator's jaw tightened. "Last warning. Drop your weapons."

A tense silence. The truckers held their breath.

Then—Bang! A shot rang out.

The Gunfight

Chaos erupted. RCMP snipers returned fire—suppressed cracks splitting the night.

One militia shooter crumpled, blood blooming across his chest.

Another fired wildly before a bullet sent him tumbling onto the pavement.

Danner and the last standing American bolted for the treeline. "Damn it!" Danner hissed, dragging his wounded ally toward the ditch.

They had one shot left. Cross the Red River. Slip into Minnesota. Disappear.

The Escape

The fugitives stumbled across the ice. Breathless. Bleeding. Desperate.

They reached the Minnesota side just as flashing lights appeared. But not RCMP lights.

Minnesota State Troopers. "Hands where we can see them!"

Danner froze, chest heaving. They were caught. Too exhausted to resist, They dropped their weapons and surrendered.

The Cover-Up

Washington, D.C. – FBI Headquarters

The Director sat alone, a dim light casting shadows across his desk.

The phone rang once. He picked it up. "They're in custody," a voice reported.

A pause.

Then—"Not for long."

A second call was made.

One hour later—Danner and his accomplice were quietly released. No paperwork. No mugshots. No record they were ever there.

By morning, they had vanished.

As far as the U.S. government was concerned, the Red River Skirmish had never happened.

But in Canada—The truth was out. Two dead Americans. A shattered border.

A growing realization. This wasn't just a trade war anymore. This was something worse. And this—was just the beginning.

The Prime Minister's Office – Ottawa

The tension in the Prime Minister's Office was suffocating. The air crackled with urgency.

Prime Minister Geneviève Lacroix sat at the head of the long conference table; her face unreadable.

To her right sat RCMP Commissioner Alex Lafontaine, his sharp eyes betraying no emotion. He was a man who had seen too much—and tonight, he had seen too much again.

Across from him, Chief of Staff Robin Hay jotted notes, his pen moving swiftly. The large screen at the end of the room displayed several government officials joining via secure video link—the Manitoba Premier, key Cabinet

Ministers, and Intelligence officers monitoring the fallout.

Lacroix folded her hands on the table. "Let's hear it, Commissioner."

The Briefing

Lafontaine nodded. "At 18:45 local time, the RCMP Emergency Response Team neutralized an armed threat blocking Highway 75. Two deceased. American nationals."

He exhaled. "No ID. No fingerprints in our system. Nothing. Their bodies are en route to Winnipeg for forensic examination, but so far? They're ghosts."

The Manitoba Premier, visibly rattled, leaned forward on the screen. "Jesus Christ. Armed Americans running a rogue checkpoint on our soil?"

Lafontaine nodded. "They were trying to create a spectacle.-mOur sources believe this was orchestrated to provoke a response."

Chief of Staff Robin Hay exhaled sharply. "And they got exactly what they wanted."

The Call from Washington

A secure line rang on the Prime Minister's desk. A direct call from Washington.

Lacroix's gaze hardened. She pressed the button.

President Jefferson Harland's voice thundered through the room. "Geneviève, what the hell is going on up there?"

His tone was fury wrapped in steel. "Two of our citizens—American hunters—just got executed by your RCMP in Manitoba. I want answers, and I want them now."

Lacroix took a steady breath. "Hunters?"

Her voice was level. Controlled. Cold. "President Harland, these men were heavily armed, blocking commercial traffic, and threatening civilians at gunpoint. My officers followed protocol."

"And now? Now, we have two dead men with no identification, no records, and no clear ties to any registered American hunters crossing into Canada."

She leaned forward, her voice slicing through the silence. "So, tell me, Mr. President—who were they really?"

Another Standoff

Silence.

Harland scoffed. "You're overreacting, Geneviève. These were two Americans legally in your country."

"Maybe they got lost. Maybe they got confused. But your people killed them in cold blood."

Lacroix's jaw clenched. "Don't insult my intelligence. They were militia, President Harland. And this has your administration's fingerprints all over it."

Harland laughed coldly. "You have no proof of that."

Lacroix's eyes darkened. "Not yet."

A sharp exhale from the other end of the line.

Then, Harland's voice shifted—Measured. Dangerous. "Regardless, we're increasing security at all northern border crossings. More Customs and Border Protection assets. National Guard presence along key corridors."

Lacroix's gaze flickered with defiance. "Fine. Canada will be tightening border security, increasing intelligence operations, and expanding screening of all American nationals entering our country."

A pause. The kind of pause that means something is changing.

Harland spoke first. "So that's how this is going to be?"

Lacroix didn't blink. "It's how it has to be."

The silence stretched. A diplomatic Mexican standoff.

Finally—

Harland muttered, "Then I guess I'll see you at the next summit."

The line went dead.

Aftermath

Lacroix leaned back in her chair.

Her hands clasped together as she surveyed the room.

RCMP Commissioner Lafontaine spoke first. "We just stepped into something bigger than we realized."

Lacroix nodded slowly. "And it's only the beginning. The war is no longer just economic. It is political. It is territorial. It is personal."

16

UNUSUAL ALLY

The Hallway Encounter

Lenny Bishop carried his groceries through the apartment building's main lobby, balancing the weight as he stepped into the elevator. He exhaled, shifting the bags to one arm, and pressed the button for his floor.

The doors slid open, and he stepped out, turning right toward his apartment.

Then he heard it. A faint creak. The stairwell door.

Lenny kept walking, keeping his posture relaxed, but every nerve in his body went taut. Someone had followed him. And whoever it was, they were trying to be quiet about it.

His instincts kicked in. A smell—body soap. Close. Too close.

Lenny dropped his groceries and spun. The flat of his palm struck a face hard. The impact sent the figure stumbling back with a grunt, a splash of blood darkening the hallway floor.

"Fuck, Lenny! What the fuck!" The voice was familiar.

Lenny stepped back, assessing the damage. The man clutched his face, blood running between his fingers—Ethan Cole.

Lenny exhaled; his adrenaline still high. He hadn't seen Cole in months and certainly hadn't expected him to show up unannounced.

"What the hell are you doing here, Cole?" Lenny demanded. His tone was cold, controlled. "Sneaking up behind me? I told you to stay away. You deaf or just stupid?"

Cole spat blood, checking his teeth with his tongue. "Goddamn, Bishop. You always greet people like this?"

Before Lenny could answer, a door opened down the hall.

Natalie Cheng stepped out, her eyes immediately locking onto the blood on Cole's face. "What happened?" she asked, her voice sharp.

Neither man answered.

Her gaze flickered to Lenny, her expression turning accusatory. "You hit him, didn't you?"

Lenny shrugged. "Instinct."

Natalie scowled and pulled Cole inside her apartment, grabbing his arm. "Come on," she said.

Lenny hesitated, then followed them in.

Secrets in the Dark

Natalie worked quickly, cleaning the blood from Cole's mouth.

"You're lucky," she muttered. "Lenny didn't hit you full on—just enough to mess up your mouth. Your nose is fine, but you've got a couple of loose teeth."

Cole winced. "Yeah. Real lucky." He shot Lenny a glare.

Lenny crossed his arms, standing by the door. "You're still not telling me why you're here, Cole. And if you don't start talking, I might just finish what I started."

Cole wiped his mouth, his expression darkening. "They killed my friend."

Silence.

Lenny's stance shifted slightly. "Who?"

"A contact in Belarus. He was CIA—one of ours. His name was leaked by Harland's administration."

Natalie's face paled.

"No one knows who killed him," Cole continued, his voice tight, "but I do."

Lenny exhaled slowly. "So, Harland's people are getting CIA agents killed now?"

Cole nodded. "And it's worse than that. Names are still being leaked. The Agency's database has been locked down for decades, but now Harland's inner circle—Winthrop's crew—have been getting access. Presidential orders."

Natalie looked at Lenny. "Why would he do that?"

Cole's expression hardened. "Because Harland's not running a democracy anymore. He's running an autocracy."

Lenny stayed silent, letting that settle.

Cole leaned forward. "Harland's administration isn't collapsing—it's consolidating power. Elections still happen, but the game is rigged. Media control is tightening. Oligarchs are being given free rein in exchange for loyalty. Harland and his backers are turning the U.S. into a corporate-run autocracy."

Natalie's hands clenched. "And the CIA?"

Cole exhaled. "We're in trouble. Harland's people don't want an independent intelligence agency. They want a loyal one. Anyone they can't control is being sidelined—or worse."

Lenny sat down. "And what do you want?"

Cole pulled a flash drive from his jacket and set it on the table. "To bring Harland down."

Lenny studied the drive.

"That flash drive contains proof that the Red River Border Skirmish was orchestrated from the highest levels of Harland's administration." Cole's voice was steady. "Not just an operation gone wrong. A deliberate attack. Harland's inner circle used a radicalized militia to create a crisis—one they could use to justify militarizing the border and expanding executive powers."

Natalie inhaled sharply. "And you have evidence?"

Cole nodded. "Internal communications. Orders traced back to the FBI Director's office. Carver himself signed off on it."

Lenny's mind worked fast. If that was true... it was treason.

Natalie looked at Lenny. "We need to take this to the press."

"No." Cole's voice was sharp. "We need to take it to the RCMP. You have connections. Get this into the right hands. Let them verify it. Let them act."

Lenny narrowed his eyes. "And you? Why not do it yourself?"

Cole leaned back. "I can't. I'm still an active asset in the U.S. If I make a direct move, I'm dead. But you? You're outside of their reach."

Lenny sat in silence for a moment. He didn't trust Cole—but the evidence was too big to ignore.

Finally, he asked, "What's the endgame here?"

Cole met his gaze. "We link the TNSF movement to the Pro-Democracy Movement. We use this to push for impeachment. We bring the fight to Congress and force a Senate trial."

Lenny shook his head. "That's a long shot."

Cole's eyes burned with conviction. "It's the only shot. Harland isn't worried about democracy anymore. If we don't act, he'll make sure no one can."

Lenny glanced at Natalie, then at the flash drive.

This wasn't just politics anymore. This was war. And they had just been handed the smoking gun.

One Last Fight

That night, Lenny sat alone in his apartment, the weight of everything pressing down on him.

The cancer had been creeping in for months, sapping his energy, gnawing at his body. The doctor's words echoed in his head. "Stage IV metastatic bladder cancer. One to three years."

But Lenny had already decided—he wasn't going to spend his last years sitting around, waiting to die. He grabbed his phone and dialled a number he hadn't used in years.

The voice on the other end was older, rougher, but still unmistakable. "Bishop? What the hell are you calling me for?"

Lenny smirked, leaning back in his chair. "Hey, McDavid.. You want to make trouble?"

A pause. Then a chuckle. "Depends. What kind of trouble are we talking about?"

Lenny exhaled, his grip tightening around the phone. "The kind that makes history."

Reggie

The Weight of Procrastination

Months had passed since Lenny had told his eldest son, Randy, that he'd check in on Reggie. But as always, he procrastinated when it came to things that made him uncomfortable.

Now, standing outside the sports bar on a cool autumn night, Lenny exhaled sharply before stepping inside.

The dimly lit bar smelled of old beer and fryer grease. The hum of conversation blended with the crackle of a hockey game on the overhead screens. At a corner booth, slumped over a half-empty glass, sat Reggie.

His youngest son looked up as Lenny approached. Bloodshot eyes. Unshaven face. Shoulders hunched under the weight of something heavier than exhaustion. "Lenny," Reggie muttered, barely looking up. He rarely called him Dad anymore.

Lenny slid into the seat across from him, resting his hands on the sticky table. "Been a while."

Reggie smirked bitterly. "Yeah. Thought you'd forgotten about me."

Lenny leaned forward, lowering his voice. "I didn't forget, Reg. I've just been... busy."

Reggie scoffed, taking a sip of his beer. "Right. Your movement or whatever it is."

Lenny ignored the sarcasm. He studied his son carefully, noting the slight tremor in his fingers, the weight of disappointment in his posture. "How's work?"

Reggie chuckled dryly. "Work? What work? Got laid off last month. Manufacturing's drying up because of the damn tariffs. Boss said they might call me back if things turn around." He shrugged. "Not holding my breath."

Lenny sighed. "You're staying at a buddy's place, right?"

"Yeah. Couch-surfing. It's fine." But the look in Reggie's eyes said otherwise.

They sat in silence for a while, the sound of the game filling the space between them. It wasn't perfect, but it was a start.

Father and Son

Reggie swirled what was left of his beer, watching the foam settle. "So, what's really going on, Lenny? Why do you look like the weight of the worlds on your shoulders?"

Lenny exhaled, rubbing his face. He glanced around, making sure no one was listening. Then, leaning in, he spoke in a muffled voice.

"I just handed the RCMP something big. Something that could bring down the President of the United States."

Reggie blinked. "Wait—what?"

Lenny sighed. "Long story. But if this goes the way I think it will… things are about to get a hell of a lot worse before they get better."

Reggie stared at him for a long moment, then shook his head with a humourless laugh. "Jesus, Lenny. You always did know how to pick a fight."

Lenny smirked. "Guess I did."

They clinked their glasses together in silent understanding.

For the first time in years, it felt like they were speaking the same language.

But Lenny knew something Reggie didn't.

He hid the visible signs. He dosed himself with opioids before coming, keeping the pain at bay. He wore loose clothing to disguise the weight loss. And when people noticed his shrinking appetite, he'd brush it off—

"I grabbed a snack earlier" or "TNSF is running me ragged."

But Reggie was sharp in his own way. He'd see through the act if Lenny wasn't careful.

An Envelope of Silence

Lenny reached into his pocket, pulled out a thick envelope, and slid it across the table.

"There's a couple thousand in there. Get yourself a place. When you run out, let me know. I'll give you more."

Reggie stared at the envelope, then up at his father. Tears welled in his eyes.

"You don't have to do this. Where's all this money coming from?"

Lenny shrugged, forcing a half-smile. "Government pensions. And those silly books I write—they actually sell. I'd rather you have the money."

He knew he was enabling him. Every expert on addiction would tell him to put the money in a trust—to make Reggie earn it, to distribute it when he was sober.

But Lenny didn't have time for the right way. He only had time to make things easier for his son.

They didn't talk much after that. If they did, the conversation would have been a mess of regrets—"I'm sorry." "You shouldn't have." "If only I could."

All the things that get said too late, when the bond between a father and son has never been solid.

Instead, Lenny reached across the table, placed his hand over Reggie's, and looked at him—really looked at him—trying to show love without letting the tears come.

After a moment, he got up. He tossed money on the table—enough to cover lunch, enough to cover Reggie's next round.

He placed a hand on his son's shoulder. "I love you, kid." Then he left, knowing it was the last time he'd ever see him.

The Late-Night News

That night, Lenny sat alone in his apartment, a beer untouched in front of him.

The television flickered with the late-night news.

Prime Minister Lacroix addressed the nation, her face solemn but defiant.

"... President Harland's threat to annex Canada is real driven by his hunger for the country's critical minerals.

Lenny scoffed. Why should I give a shit?

But something inside him refused to let it go. His spirit pushed back.

Everything he had left—his time, his strength, his money—would be spent fighting that fucking asshole, Harland.

No matter what it cost.

17

A CHAMPION SPEAKS

Prime Minister Geneviève Lacroix's Address to the American People and the World

[Broadcast on National and International Networks]

My friends,

I speak to you today not just as the Prime Minister of Canada, but as a representative of a nation bound to yours by history, trade, and an enduring friendship that has withstood the test of time.

On September 11, 2001, as the United States faced an unthinkable act of terror, the world watched in horror—but we, your Canadian neighbours, acted.

In the small town of Gander, Newfoundland and Labrador, thousands of passengers were forced to land when American airspace closed. Homes and hearts were opened. Canadians welcomed strangers with warmth, shelter, and food.

We did what friends do—we stood by you in your darkest hour, just as you have stood by us when we needed you.

This friendship has been reinforced not only by shared values but by deep economic ties.

Since the landmark free trade agreement of the 1980s, modernized in 2018, Canada and the United States have built one of the most integrated economic partnerships in the world:

> ✔ Nearly $1.4 trillion in trade crosses our border each year.
> ✔ 400,000 people travel between our countries every day.
> ✔ Canadian Snowbirds contribute $22 billion annually to local U.S. economies.

But my friends, something has changed.

This so-called "tariff war" was started on false pretenses—a war that has not only strained our economies but has hurt ordinary Americans and Canadians alike.

You were told that fentanyl from Canada was flooding into your country. Yet the latest intelligence shows:

✗ Over 90% of fentanyl enters the U.S. from China and Mexico—not from Canada.

✗ Illegal immigration across our shared border is a fraction of what moves through your southern frontier.

✗ Most illegal firearms in Canada originate from the United States.

Despite these facts, Canada has acted in good faith.

We have invested $6 billion in enhanced border security to prevent this trade war from escalating further.

And yet, the tariffs remain.

The result?

📉 Canadian pensions eroding.
📈 Inflation rising.
📉 Unemployment climbing.
📈 American businesses losing reliable supply chains.

We have held back on retaliatory measures against U.S. energy needs— but if forced, we will reconsider.

🇨🇦 Canada supplies over 60% of your imported crude oil and a majority of your natural gas from foreign sources. Cutting that off is not a decision we take lightly.

But watching our own economy be choked under baseless tariffs?

That is not a decision we will accept.

Now, I come to the real reason I am speaking to you today.

The Red River Border Skirmish.

This past November, in a tragic escalation, two American citizens were shot by the RCMP near the border.

I wish that were the whole story. It is not.

(*Prime Minister Lacroix holds up a small flash drive.*)

On this drive are emails, text messages, and direct communications showing that FBI Director Carver was involved in planning and approving this attack on Canadian sovereignty.

- ✔ This was no accident.
- ✔ It was orchestrated.

And while I cannot yet tell you that your President was behind it—I ask you to consider the possibility.

A Global Reckoning

I will be addressing the United Nations General Assembly from my office here in Ottawa.

The Secretary-General already has a copy of this evidence. The world will see the truth.

And so, my American friends, I ask you to look beyond the rhetoric, beyond the distractions.

There are those within your government laying the groundwork to annex Canada—To take what is not theirs, through manufactured crises and economic sabotage.

A Nation Unbroken

Let me be clear:

🇨🇦 Canada does not have the might to fight a war to preserve what we have.

But I say this with absolute conviction—Nothing has ever united Canadians more than the threat of losing our sovereignty. We will not go quietly.

The world is watching.

And I trust that, even now, the true American spirit—the one that has long championed freedom, justice, and the right of all nations to determine their own destiny—will rise again.

Thank you.

[Broadcast Ends]

The Oval Office – Watching Lacroix's Speech

The Oval Office is silent except for the crisp, unwavering voice of Prime Minister Geneviève Lacroix on the massive screen. The room's three occupants—President Jefferson Harland, Chief of Staff Maggie Kellerman, and billionaire

Grant Winthrop—watch with sharp focus as Lacroix raises the flash drive for the world to see.

The speech ends.

Harland explodes.

Harland (furious): "That goddamn woman just declared war on us on live television!"

His fist slams against the Resolute Desk, rattling the crystal water glass beside him. His face is red, his breathing heavy.

Across from him, Maggie Kellerman remains still, composed as always, her hands clasped in front of her. Grant Winthrop, on the other hand, leans back in his chair, a small, thoughtful smile playing on his lips.

Harland (seething): "She just threatened to cut off our goddamn energy supply! She's accusing my administration of plotting against Canada! This is an act of hostility, and she did it on our airwaves! On our networks!"

Winthrop (calm, assessing): "She's good."

Harland snaps his glare toward him.

Harland: "What the hell do you mean, she's good?"

Winthrop adjusts his cufflinks, his voice smooth.

Winthrop: "She didn't come at you directly. She planted doubt. That's a smart play. It's not about proving anything—

it's about making the world wonder if it's true. She framed it perfectly: she's the reasonable leader, appealing to the people, while we're the aggressors pulling strings behind the scenes."

Harland: "So, what do we do? We can't let this stand. Do I go on TV tonight? Address the nation? Call this what it is—a desperate, pathetic attempt to slander me?"

Kellerman finally speaks, her voice controlled, deliberate.

Kellerman: "You need to think this through, Mr. President. A direct response elevates her. It makes this a battle between two heads of state. She wants that."

Harland: "So, we just let her get away with it?"

Kellerman shakes her head.

Kellerman: "No. We respond—just not the way she wants us to. First, we push our UN Ambassador to address the General Assembly, dismissing her so-called 'evidence' as 'AI-generated propaganda, fabricated to frame the United States.' Make it about deepfakes, about foreign interference. We cast doubt, muddy the waters. The moment we admit this flash drive has any legitimacy, we lose ground."

Harland exhales, considering.

Harland: "Alright. What else?"

Kellerman leans forward slightly.

Kellerman: "We don't just fight back in public. We go after her at home. Push our operatives in Canada to unearth dirt on opposition party members and key Premiers. We don't need to discredit her directly—we just need Canadians to demand an election. Frame her as the reckless leader who is mishandling relations with the United States. Create a movement calling for new leadership."

A slow smirk spreads across Winthrop's face.

Winthrop: "Force her to fight on two fronts—against us and against her own political system. Make her defend herself from within."

Harland exhales sharply, his fury shifting into something colder, more calculated.

Harland: "Do it. I want every goddamn lever pulled. Lacroix wants to play on the world stage. Let's see how well she holds up under real pressure."

The war for control has begun.

Pro Democracy Movement (PDM)

Raul Perez stood before a small but devoted gathering of PDM followers, his voice charged with conviction. It was moments after the Canadian Prime Minister had addressed the American people directly—a seismic event that would ripple through the political landscape.

"Folks, what happened tonight? That was *us*." His eyes scanned the room, his words deliberate. "That flash drive had *our* fingerprints all over it. The administration thought they could purge the FBI and expect good, honest officers and civilian members not to remain? *They* are our eyes and ears. *They* are the reason the truth is getting out."

He paused, letting the gravity of his words settle.

"We must be relentless. We must be persuasive. The American people must understand—Harland's administration isn't just a threat to our democracy. It's a threat to the world order.

"There isn't a single nation on this planet, not even China, that can stand toe-to-toe with the United States. That's what makes this so dangerous. Harland doesn't care about our historical allies. He doesn't listen. He *bullies* the world into submission. And why? Because he and Winthrop believe the world should be ruled by the elite—by the wealthy, the powerful, the untouchable."

His voice hardened.

"But hear me now—his downfall, *their* downfall, won't come from foreign powers. It won't come from the press or from politicians afraid to take a stand. No, it will come from an *American* movement. A movement like ours. A movement that works *within* the law to bring him to his knees."

The room erupted in applause, hands clapping, voices rising. A few reached out, gripping his shoulder, slapping his back.

The fight was far from over. But tonight, they had won a battle.

18

THE LETTER CAMPAIGN

Mobilizing the Movement

TNSF researchers estimated that at least 5-7 million people in both Canada and the U.S. had direct family ties—a parent, sibling, or first cousin—on the other side of the border. Millions more had close friends, professional relationships, and business interests tied between the two nations.

The solution? A letter campaign.

A carefully crafted message—personal yet powerful—encouraging Canadians to reach out to their American family and friends, urging them to push back against the tariffs.

Letters could be sent electronically or the old-fashioned way—stamped, sealed, and mailed.

Example Letter

Hey Sis,

I need to talk to you about something that's been weighing on me.

You know how we've always been more than just neighbours —how Canadians and Americans have looked out for each other, through thick and thin? That's what family does.

But lately, it doesn't feel like that. The people running your country aren't treating us like friends anymore.

These tariffs? They're crushing us. Prices are skyrocketing, jobs are disappearing, and families are feeling it in ways that go way beyond politics. And the worst part? It's like we don't even matter to them.

I know this isn't you. This isn't the America I grew up trusting—the one that stood with us, just like we've always stood with you. I don't want to see that change.

So, I'm asking—not as a Canadian, not as someone on the other side of the border—but as your brother. Pay attention to what's happening. Speak up if you can. Because this isn't just about Canada.

It's about the kind of world we want to live in.

Love,
Your Brother Up North
Melfort, Saskatchewan

Taking the Fight to Small-Town Canada

The drive from Regina to Melfort was brutal.

Wind howled across the open prairie, lifting walls of snow into blinding whiteouts that swallowed the road. The temperature had plummeted to a bone-shattering minus forty with the windchill.

Natalie gripped the steering wheel, her eyes locked on the faint red glow of taillights ahead—the only thing guiding her forward.

Lenny sat in the passenger seat, unusually quiet, rubbing his cold, stiff hands together despite the car's blasting heater.

"Remind me why we're doing this again?" he muttered, his breath fogging the window.

"Because we have to," Natalie said, her voice tight with focus. "People need to know they have a way to fight back."

Lenny exhaled slowly. "I just hope they're ready to listen."

The Town Hall—A Nation Awakens

After three gruelling hours, they reached Melfort. The town, buried under thick snowdrifts, was eerily quiet, save for the occasional whine of the wind.

A local TNSF representative met them at the town hall—a 500-seat venue.

But as they entered, the sound hit them first—a deep hum of conversation, thick with urgency.

The hall was overflowing. At least 600 people had crammed inside—standing shoulder to shoulder, lining the back walls, filling the aisles.

As the Canadian flag was raised, the entire crowd stood and burst into O Canada, their voices raw, defiant, unshaken.

The air crackled with something powerful. Something unstoppable.

When Natalie was introduced, the ovation was deafening.

Natalie Takes the Stage

She stepped up to the mic, heart pounding, eyes scanning the faces before her.

"Thank you."

"We're here tonight because we are DONE being pushed around."

"The United States has started a phoney tariff war against us —not against our government, not against the corporations, but against YOU. Against your families, your businesses, your way of life.

And we are not going to take it lying down."

A ripple of agreement ran through the crowd.

She gestured to lists they had distributed—Canadian-made, Canadian-produced goods, alternatives to American imports. She held up pamphlets detailing free legal and financial advisors to help people divest from U.S. properties, stocks, and bonds.

"This isn't about politics. This is about survival. And if they think they can strangle us into submission, they've underestimated Canadians.

We are not just neighbours to the United States—we are a NATION. And we will stand on our own."

The crowd erupted. People nodded in agreement, flipped through the pamphlets, and clapped so hard their hands ached.

Lenny's Moment—And Collapse

Then it was Lenny's turn.

"We've been through tough times before."

"We survived depressions, recessions, wars, and political fights that could have torn us apart. But every single time, we got back up. Because that's who we are."

"But make no mistake—this is a fight. And we either face it together, or we let them walk all over us."

Applause surged through the room.

But then—something changed.

Lenny's breath hitched. His grip on the podium tightened. Then—his legs gave out.

Gasps ripped through the hall.

Someone shouted, "Natalie!" She was already moving, rushing to his side.

His face was deathly pale, beads of sweat forming despite the freezing air.

"Call an ambulance!"

Minutes later, Lenny was being rushed to Melfort Hospital.

Natalie rode beside him, gripping his hand, willing him to stay with her. "Lenny," she whispered urgently. "What's wrong?"

His eyes fluttered open briefly. With a weak smile, he murmured, "Guess I should've told you sooner."

The Truth—Lenny's Secret Battle

In the hospital room, machines beeped softly.

Natalie sat beside Lenny's bed, arms wrapped tightly around herself, bracing for impact. "Stage IV?" she repeated, her voice barely above a whisper.

Lenny nodded. "It's spread to my lymph nodes. Maybe further."

Her stomach twisted. "How long?"

"A few months. A year if I'm lucky."

She shook her head. "And you weren't going to tell me?"

Lenny exhaled, rubbing his temples. "What would you have done? Made me quit? Stopped me from doing what I believe in?"

"Yes," she snapped. "I would've stopped you. I would've made you take care of yourself instead of running yourself into the ground."

A small, tired smile tugged at his lips. "And that's exactly why I didn't tell you."

The doctor entered then, clipboard in hand. "Mr. Bishop, you were lucky this time. But your body is sending a clear message—you need to slow down."

Lenny chuckled, though it came out as more of a rasp. "That's not happening, Doc."

The doctor sighed. "I figured as much. But at the very least, listen to your body. Because next time, you might not wake up."

The Argument

The drive back to Regina was thick with tension. Snow swirled across the highway, but Natalie's grip on the wheel had nothing to do with the weather. "You need to stop, Lenny," she said finally.

"No."

"Lenny, you collapsed in front of six hundred people. Your body is screaming at you to slow down."

"I'm not quitting," he said, staring out at the endless prairie. "Not now. Not when people need us."

"People need you alive, Lenny!"

He turned to her, his eyes heavy with exhaustion but filled with the same unshakable resolve. "I have cancer, Natalie. Whether I stop or not, it doesn't change that. But at least this way, I matter."

Her throat tightened. "And what happens when you collapse again? When you don't get back up?"

He smiled faintly. "Then I guess I go down fighting."

Natalie swallowed hard, her heart aching. She wanted to scream, to make him see reason. But she knew Lenny too well. He wasn't backing down.

So, she said nothing.

She just kept driving—through the cold, through the dark, through the endless stretch of prairie, toward a future she wasn't ready to face.

19

CANADIAN POLITICS

The Virtual Meeting

Prime Minister Geneviève Lacroix sat in her office in Ottawa, a steaming cup of black coffee untouched on her desk. The virtual meeting was moments away. On her screen, dozens of faces were waiting—every federal parliamentarian, every provincial premier, and every First Nations and Métis leader. The weight of their collective gaze pressed upon her, some expectant, others defiant.

She had fought hard to keep Canada intact in this trade war with the United States. Her strategy, rallying a unified *Team Canada*, had been strong at first. But as the months wore on, cracks had begun to show. Some provincial premiers, under mounting pressure from businesses and political donors, were pushing for a softer stance with President Harland's administration. A few were even entertaining the unthinkable—the idea that Canada might be better off as part of the United States.

One premier had already crossed the line. The Canadian Security Intelligence Agency (CSIS) had briefed her days ago: this man had secretly opened back channels with Washington, discussing what an *annexation* could look like. He wasn't just a critic. He was a traitor. And he wasn't alone.

The calls for her resignation were growing louder—from opposition leaders and from within her own party. Her approval ratings had plunged, but her recent televised speech to the American people had given her a second wind. It had been a gamble, but it had paid off. For now.

Tonight, her message had to be clear.

She tapped the unmute button and leaned forward.

"Good evening," she began, her voice steady. "Let me be absolutely clear: Canada's sovereignty is *not* for sale."

A pause. The silence stretched.

"I know some of you believe that easing tensions with the United States means making concessions, that giving ground will bring peace. I am telling you now—anyone who negotiates away our sovereignty, who goes behind the government's back to speak with foreign officials about our future, will face severe consequences."

Some shifted uncomfortably in their seats. Others watched her with impassive expressions.

"I will not hesitate to take action against those who betray this country," she continued, her tone sharpening. "If you are a member of my party and you are caught in backdoor dealings with Washington, you will be immediately expelled from caucus. You will lose your political career, your influence, and your allies."

She let those words sink in before pressing forward.

"If these negotiations involve illegal activity—bribery, foreign interference, actions that undermine national security—you will not just face political consequences. You will face criminal investigation by the RCMP and CSIS."

A murmur rippled through the call.

"There will be no anonymity for those working against Canada. If necessary, I will expose names publicly. The people of this country deserve to know who is putting their future at risk."

She turned to the premiers, her gaze piercing.

"If you are a premier, and you are actively working to weaken our position, understand this: your province's federal funding is *not* guaranteed. Equalization payments, infrastructure investments, emergency relief—these are *conditional* on good governance. If you undermine Canada, don't expect Ottawa to fund it."

One of the premiers, a man who had been vocally critical of her trade policies, shifted in his chair. Good. He had heard her loud and clear.

"And if any province chooses to go further—if it acts in a way that directly threatens national unity—I will invoke the *Emergencies Act* to protect this country."

Her words landed like a hammer.

She turned to the First Nations and Métis leaders.

"To our Indigenous leaders, I say this: sovereignty matters. *Your* sovereignty matters. But there are those who would exploit it, who would use it as a bargaining chip for their own gain. If I find that any Indigenous leaders are negotiating with foreign powers in a way that threatens Canada, I will suspend treaty negotiations and financial agreements until we ensure that the interests of *all* Indigenous communities—not just a select few—are truly represented."

Another pause. She had more to say.

"This is not just about internal politics. If a *foreign government* is involved in any of this, they will face diplomatic retaliation. Their ambassadors will be expelled. Their influence in Canada will be reduced. And if trade is being used as a weapon, we will respond in kind. We will halt agreements, fortify our security, and defend our economic independence."

She exhaled, letting the weight of her words settle over the call.

"Canada has stood for over 150 years because leaders before us had the courage to defend it. I intend to do the same. If any of you doubt my resolve, *test me*."

She ended the call.

For a moment, silence filled the room. Then she reached for her coffee, now cold, and took a sip.

Private Briefing: The State of the Nation

Robin Hay stepped into Lacroix's office, the scent of fresh coffee trailing behind him. Across the room, Julia Fortier, the head of CSIS, sat at a small table, already deep in discussion with the Prime Minister.

Hay set down a tray of Tim Hortons cups, their lids barely containing the steam curling into the air. He kept one for himself, setting it down before waving his hands, trying to cool them after carrying the scalding cups.

Lacroix leaned forward; expression unreadable. "We've received overtures from China for closer relations."

Fortier exhaled sharply. "Yeah, and that would *guarantee* an American invasion."

Hay silently took notes, his pen scratching against the pad.

Fortier continued, her voice edged with frustration. "Your UN address was effective in rallying countries like Denmark—because they fear the U.S. will annex Greenland. And, of course, China played its usual card, condemning American imperialism. But England, Germany, France... they've been frustratingly reserved. They're afraid of Harland. Brazil and Argentina *want* to push back against him, but they've barely returned our calls. We're cornered."

Lacroix folded her hands. "Are we reaching out to the Pro-Democracy Movement?"

Fortier shook her head. "Too dangerous. The CIA has operatives scattered throughout Canada. If we're seen supporting the PDM, it'll be *us* condemned at the UN. Worse, it could provoke an American crackdown, branding them as foreign collaborators."

She hesitated, then added, "That said, we have *one* open channel—through a CIA agent in Regina. Only Inspector McDavid and two TNSF workers know of him. Now, you two do as well."

She fixed them both with a hard stare. "You must never speak his name to anyone."

Lacroix nodded. "Understood. Is there anything we need to pass along to him?"

"No," Fortier replied firmly. "We'll receive intelligence through this channel, then decide how to disseminate it—to inform our people and the world, just like we did with the Red River Border incident."

She exhaled, rubbing her temples. "There's a growing number of Canadian business leaders secretly discussing pulling out—shutting down operations here and relocating to the U.S. if you cut the subsidies. At the same time, investment funds are seeing massive withdrawals. Canadians don't trust their money is safe, and foreign investors see better returns elsewhere. Our stock market is in free-fall—back to where it was during the 2008 financial crisis."

Lacroix let out a bitter laugh. "Thanks for the good news."

When the others left, Hay lingered. Lacroix avoided his gaze, staring at her coffee.

Then, in a quiet voice, she murmured, "Maybe I should resign."

Hay didn't hesitate. "Canadians need you, Geneviève. *You're the one who can save this country.*"

She swallowed hard, then nodded.

She wasn't going anywhere.

20

THE FBI'S SHIFT – CANADA AS AN "ENEMY"

Washington, D.C. – FBI Headquarters

The air inside FBI Headquarters was thick with tension. President Harland sat at the head of the long conference table, his fingers drumming against the polished wood. Across from him sat FBI Director Dale Carver, the hard-nosed former sheriff who had built his career on cracking down on *un-American elements.*

Harland's presidency was unraveling.

A year ago, he had imposed a crushing 25% tariff on Canadian imports, expecting Prime Minister Geneviève Lacroix to cave. Instead, she had negotiated it down to 10%, making him look weak.

Now, his poll numbers were in free fall.

Southern red states—his own base—were calling for reconciliation with Canada, as their industries suffered under retaliatory tariffs. The *Pro-Democracy Movement (PDM)* in the U.S. was still alive, despite the FBI's efforts to dismantle it. Great Britain and the European Community were hammering him over trade, and now the CIA was warning that China was growing closer to Canada.

And then there was Winthrop.

Douglas Winthrop, his *right-hand person*, was dominating the headlines, overshadowing Harland on foreign policy. Pundits whispered that he was the real Commander-in-Chief, not Harland.

Harland's hands clenched into fists. *That bastard.*

He needed an enemy—a new target to shift the narrative.

His eyes locked onto Carver.

"It's time to turn the screws."

Carver leaned forward, a smirk tugging at the corner of his mouth. "How far do you want to go?"

Harland's voice was ice.

"I want *True North Strong and Free* labeled as a foreign subversive organization. I want them treated as collaborators—shut down their fundraising, cut their access to American institutions, and make life impossible for their members. And I want this done immediately."

Carver nodded. "We can work with that."

The FBI's Response

Within hours, the Bureau shifted focus.

- Canadian nationals tied to *True North Strong and Free* were quietly banned from entering the U.S. without explanation.
- Financial transactions involving the organization and U.S. institutions were flagged and delayed or outright denied.
- American-based social media platforms began restricting accounts suspected of spreading pro-Canadian messaging.
- Journalists covering the movement faced increased scrutiny at border crossings, with some detained for hours under vague *national security concerns*.
- U.S. intelligence agencies leaned on allied security services, feeding them leads to increase monitoring of Canadian activists abroad.

But what Harland didn't know was that Prime Minister Lacroix had already been warned.

Ottawa – Prime Minister's Office

The report arrived in a sealed envelope, funnelled through the Regina back channel—the same secret pipeline that had delivered intelligence from an FBI mole to the *Pro-Democracy Movement* in the U.S. The message was clear: Harland had met with the FBI. A crackdown was coming.

Lacroix read the briefing in silence; her face unreadable. Then, she turned to her chief of staff.

"Strengthen our security for internal communications and inform TNSF to do the same," she ordered. "Warn all those being targeted to watch for surveillance and report any signs of it to the police immediately."

Her voice was calm. Measured. She had been expecting this.

The pressure was mounting, but Canada would not bend.

21

THE TRIUMVIRATE CRUMBLES

The Oval Office – The Move Against Winthrop

President Jefferson Harland leaned back in his leather chair, his fingers steepled beneath his chin. The Oval Office, once a sanctuary of power, felt smaller now, more suffocating. The monitors lining the far wall fed him a constant stream of news and intelligence, and it was all the same: *Winthrop, Winthrop, Winthrop.*

The billionaire's name had become synonymous with American governance—more so than Harland's own. That realization made the president's gut churn.

Grant Winthrop had never run for office, had never won a single vote, yet he controlled the levers of power more effectively than Harland ever could. Contracts—defence, infrastructure, intelligence, even state functions—had all been funnelled through Winthrop's vast empire. His AI networks had replaced entire agencies, his technology embedded into every function of the government.

At first, Harland had welcomed the efficiency. But now? The power dynamic had shifted, and Harland could feel himself slipping into irrelevance. And worst of all, Winthrop didn't even seem to notice—or care.

Harland's Chief of Staff, Margaret Kellerman, stood in the doorway. He gestured for her to enter.

"You've seen the latest reports?" she asked.

Harland let out a slow breath. "Tell me something I don't already know."

She hesitated. "Winthrop's network is expanding into the State Department. His AI systems are replacing diplomatic personnel in key embassies."

Harland scoffed. "Security? He's embedding himself deeper into the government."

"The contracts were approved."

"The contracts were forced through," Harland corrected, leaning forward. His voice was sharp now, his anger slipping through. "He's playing both sides—striking deals with our allies and adversaries. But let's be clear, Margaret: he *owns* this administration."

She remained silent.

Harland studied her carefully. "Are you on my side, Margaret?"

Kellerman blinked once but didn't flinch. "I serve the office of the president."

A diplomatic answer. A safe answer. A useless answer.

Harland turned back to his monitors. Winthrop was on the screen, delivering a speech at a private event filled with industry titans, foreign dignitaries, and senators. He spoke with effortless confidence, exuding control.

Harland's fingers curled into a fist.

"This ends tonight."

Kellerman's gaze sharpened. "What are you planning?"

Harland pressed a button on his desk. "Get me the Secret Service. Now."

The Oval Office – The Arrest Attempt

Ten minutes later, six Secret Service agents stood at attention inside the Oval Office. Harland, seated behind the Resolute Desk, eyed each of them carefully.

"You're going to bring in Grant Winthrop," Harland said flatly.

A murmur of uncertainty passed through the room, but no one spoke.

"I want him detained. Quietly. No press, no leaks. Bring him in under national security concerns. He's compromised this administration."

One of the agents, a veteran with silver at his temples, took a measured step forward. "Sir, does the Attorney General have an indictment?"

Harland's expression darkened. "I *am* the goddamn President of the United States. You have your orders."

The agents exchanged looks, but protocol was clear. Orders from the President were to be followed.

Within the hour, Winthrop's personal security detail received an urgent alert. The billionaire was still at his private event when the Secret Service arrived at the rooftop entrance of the venue, their black SUVs moving with coordinated precision.

What they didn't anticipate was Winthrop's own security force—private, elite, and just as well-trained.

As the Secret Service agents moved in, Winthrop's men countered, weapons visible but lowered in a defensive posture. A standoff ensued.

The lead agent placed a hand on his earpiece. "Mr. President, we have a situation."

Harland's voice came through, cold and sharp. "What do you mean *situation*?"

"Winthrop's security isn't backing down. They're armed, sir. They're not standing aside."

Silence stretched over the line.

Harland's pulse pounded in his ears. He knew exactly what this meant. Winthrop had built his own state within the state.

If Harland pushed this now, the situation could spiral out of control. An armed conflict in the middle of Washington, involving his own federal security forces, would be catastrophic.

Harland gritted his teeth. *Not here. Not now.*

"Stand down," he ordered.

A pause. Then, the confirmation: "Yes, sir."

Harland slammed his hand onto the desk, his fury barely contained.

Winthrop's Retaliation

Less than an hour later, Grant Winthrop entered the Oval Office, completely unbothered, as if he had been invited.

Harland didn't stand. He didn't gesture for Winthrop to sit.

The billionaire smirked. "Really, Jeff? An *arrest*? I expected more creativity from you."

Harland's voice was cold steel. "Don't think this is over."

Winthrop chuckled. "Oh, I know it's not. That's why I'll be leaving Washington for a while. A little... *strategic retreat*."

Harland's eyes narrowed. "To where?"

Winthrop grinned. "My private island, of course. No extradition, no oversight, and, most importantly... no distractions."

He turned, heading for the door, but paused just before exiting. "Oh, and Jeff?" He glanced over his shoulder, eyes glinting with something dangerously close to amusement. "Watch your back."

Then he was gone.

Harland sat in silence for a long time.

He had made his move. And now, Winthrop was making his. The war between them had officially begun.

FBI Headquarters – Washington, D.C.

Special Agent Elliot Kane had spent months walking a tightrope, feeding intelligence to the Pro-Democracy Movement (PDM) while maintaining his cover inside the FBI. The risks had only increased after the disappearance of Mark Grayson, the previous liaison to the movement.

Tonight, Kane had something bigger than anything Grayson had ever leaked. Winthrop's financial ties to the government were being severed. If PDM moved fast, they could shut down his funding, expose his corruption, and push the administration further into chaos.

But Kane wasn't just passing along evidence. He was also giving PDM a way to weaponize the truth—and the lies

Encrypted Communication – Kane to PDM

> Kane: Harland is cutting off Winthrop's funding. Treasury payments are frozen. I have the records. You need to act before they cover it up.

> Raul Perez (PDM): Confirmed?

> Kane: Yes. Also have Kellerman's emails confirming she's tracking Winthrop. A Secret Service directive to monitor him. And an unsecured phone call where Harland ranted about how he "should've had the bastard arrested."

> Perez: Jesus.

> Kane: You need to file legal action against these payments. The moment a case is opened, it will trigger an audit of all government contracts. That will keep the money frozen—and expose even more corruption.

> Perez: Done. But this isn't enough. We need to bury both.

> Kane: I have something for that too. We flood the narrative.

> Perez: Disinformation?

> Kane: Controlled disinformation. Not wild conspiracy theories—planted doubts that make both Harland and Winthrop look worse.

The PDM's Disinformation Offensive

The Pro-Democracy Movement's digital teams had been preparing for this moment. Within hours of receiving Kane's intel, two simultaneous campaigns were launched.

1. Discrediting Harland

PDM operatives leaked "classified documents"—some real, some fabricated—suggesting:

- Harland had planned to declare a national emergency to stay in power beyond his term.

- He had secretly sought asylum guarantees in Russia and Saudi Arabia in case he was forced out.
- His cognitive decline was worse than reported, with doctored but believable internal memos discussing his mental instability.

Even though none of this could be verified, it didn't have to be. It only had to feel true—and given how unstable Harland had been acting, people believed it.

2. Sabotaging Winthrop

The second prong of the attack targeted Winthrop. The leaks framed him as:

- Having secret bank accounts in China and Dubai, suggesting he was preparing to abandon the U.S.
- Colluding with foreign intelligence services—fake emails implied he had been sharing classified U.S. technology with China for personal profit.
- Plotting to have Harland removed so he could install a puppet administration.

These stories spread like wildfire—pushed through fake social media accounts, whistleblower forums, and even mainstream news outlets desperate for exclusive scoops.

By morning, both Harland and Winthrop were being bombarded with accusations, conspiracy theories, and leaks—some true, some half-true, some outright false.

The result? Chaos.

Harland's supporters saw Winthrop as a corrupt traitor, while Winthrop's allies saw Harland as a paranoid dictator on the verge of collapse. The two factions that once ruled Washington together were now at each other's throats

The Regina Channel: Canada Reacts

The encrypted package arrived at the Prime Minister's Office in Ottawa through the trusted Regina channel, the same secret intelligence link that had delivered information about the Red River Border Skirmish months earlier.

Geneviève Lacroix read the summary report; her expression unreadable as she absorbed the details.

Harland and Winthrop were no longer allies.

The U.S. Treasury was freezing payments to Winthrop's companies.

The FBI Director was hunting the mole inside his own agency.

A Secret Service directive had been issued to track Winthrop's movements.

Harland, caught in his own spiral of paranoia, had made the fatal mistake of ranting over an unsecured line.

The Prime Minister turned to Robin Hay, her Chief of Staff, "We need to move."

Hay nodded. "I'll draft a statement reinforcing our stance. If the U.S. is in chaos, Canada needs to project stability. Investors will start looking to us as an alternative."

Lacroix exhaled slowly. "We also need to prepare for retaliation. Harland is a wounded animal now."

She turned back to the report, studying the lines about Carver and the FBI purges.

"Find out if any of these displaced agents have intelligence that could be useful to us. If Harland discarded them, they might be looking for a new home."

Hay's brow lifted. "You want to recruit former FBI?"

Lacroix didn't smile, but there was a sharpness in her gaze. "Let's just say… we should offer them asylum.

Harland Wakes to a Nightmare

By the time President Harland stepped into the Oval Office, the political landscape had shifted beneath his feet.

Margaret Kellerman was waiting, holding a stack of briefing papers.

She didn't look up when he entered. "It's bad."

Harland frowned. "Define bad."

Kellerman handed him a printout. "The Treasury audit triggered by the lawsuit has already frozen several payments to Winthrop's companies. His empire is now in immediate financial distress."

Harland skimmed the report, his hands tightening. "Who filed the case?"

Kellerman's expression was neutral. "A legal firm with connections to the Pro-Democracy Movement."

Harland slammed the papers onto the desk. "So, they knew."

Kellerman nodded. "Someone inside the government leaked it."

Harland's eyes darkened. "It's that goddamn mole."

Before he could continue, a Secret Service agent stepped into the room.

"Sir, you need to see this."

Harland turned, already furious. "What now?"

The agent handed him a transcript of a phone call. His phone call. His unsecured late-night rant about Winthrop.

Harland's blood ran cold. "This... this was recorded?"

Kellerman finally looked up, her gaze assessing. "Yes, Mr. President."

Harland's hands shook with rage. "Get Carver in here. NOW.

The Noose Tightens

Elliot Kane moved carefully, every step more dangerous than the last.

The Pro-Democracy Movement had made its move. The Canadian government had received the intel.

And now? Harland was out for blood.

Kane's window for escape was closing fast. The moment Dale Carver figured out who he was? There wouldn't be a second chance.

22

DETAINED IN CHICAGO

Secondary Inspection

The queue at passport control at O'Hare International Airport moved steadily, but Natalie Cheng barely noticed. She had traveled to the United States before—enough times that she knew the drill by heart. Present the passport, answer a few questions, get the stamp, and move on.

This time was no different—or at least, that's what she thought.

She stepped forward, handed her Canadian passport to the U.S. Customs and Border Protection officer, and waited as he scanned it. "Purpose of your visit?"

"Attending the North American Economic Conference,"

Cheng replied smoothly. "I'm a speaker on the panel about technological innovations in financial markets."

The officer, a broad-shouldered man with a blank expression, flicked his gaze to her, then back to his screen. "How long will you be staying?"

"Three days," Cheng said.

There was a pause as the officer's screen refreshed, his eyes scanning over something she couldn't see. A shift in his posture—a tightening of the shoulders—made her uneasy.

"One moment," he said before reaching for his radio. "I need a supervisor at Booth 4."

Cheng's fingers curled around the strap of her handbag. This wasn't normal.

She was led away from the primary inspection area, past the long lines of travellers waiting to clear immigration. A CBP officer escorted her down a narrow hallway into a windowless room with a metal table and two chairs. There was no phone, no clock, nothing but the hum of the overhead fluorescent lights.

A few minutes later, the door opened, and a tall man in a dark suit entered. He wasn't in a CBP uniform, but his presence carried authority. He placed a folder on the table and sat across from her.

"I'm Special Agent Monroe, Department of Homeland Security," he said. "Ms. Cheng, we have reason to believe you are associated with True North Strong and Free. Are you aware that this organization is classified as an extremist anti-government group by the United States?"

Cheng's breath caught. "That's ridiculous," she said, forcing her voice to remain steady. "True North Strong and Free is a political advocacy group. It's legal in Canada."

"In Canada, maybe," Monroe replied. "But in the United States, it's classified as an extremist organization with anti-government ties. And under U.S. law, foreign nationals associated with such groups are deemed inadmissible."

Her heart pounded. "You think I'm a threat because of that?" she asked incredulously. "I'm here for a business conference, not a protest. I don't even have any active involvement with the organization."

Monroe flipped open the file. "We have records indicating otherwise. Meeting attendance. Financial contributions. Communications with known members. That's enough."

She clenched her jaw. "Then I'll voluntarily withdraw my application for entry and return to Canada. I've done nothing wrong."

Monroe's expression didn't change. "Not an option. Under Section 212(a)(3)(B) of the Immigration and Nationality Act, you're subject to mandatory expedited removal. That means you are not just being denied entry—you're being deported and banned from future travel to the U.S."

Cheng's breath came short. This wasn't just about today. This was about forever.

"You're making a mistake," she said, her voice sharper now. "I have no criminal record. I'm a business professional. I was invited to this conference. There's nothing illegal about my visit."

Monroe didn't blink. "This decision is final. You're being placed on the next flight back to Canada. You'll be escorted to a detention area until your departure."

A CBP officer stepped in, flanking her.

"I want to speak to my lawyer," Cheng said.

"You can do that when you land in Canada," Monroe replied, standing. "Your rights don't extend here."

A chill ran down her spine. This wasn't just a denial of entry. This was a targeted move—a message that she wasn't welcome in the United States.

As the officers motioned for her to stand, Cheng lifted her chin and squared her shoulders. This wasn't over. And whoever had flagged her as a threat wanted her to know it.

The Fallout

A few days later, Natalie met Ethan Cole in the university cafeteria. The place was bustling with students, the hum of conversation providing cover for their meeting. To any outsider, it looked like she was helping him with coursework—just another professor explaining something to a graduate student.

They were being cautious.

Natalie spoke in a hushed voice, recounting everything that had happened at Chicago O'Hare Airport.

"I was terrified, Ethan," she admitted, staring down at her untouched cup of coffee. "The way they looked at me—their power over me—it was humiliating. I wasn't a person to them. Just another name to be erased."

Ethan listened, his jaw tightening. "PDM's intelligence says this nightmare may be ending soon."

"Soon?" Natalie's voice cracked, her eyes glistening with unshed tears. "What does soon even mean? I was deported. I have a lifetime ban from your country. This isn't temporary for me, Ethan. It's forever."

Ethan exhaled sharply, choosing his words carefully. "A new administration will review all these bans—wipe them out. Not all of us follow Harland. This won't last."

"But soon?" she pressed. "Harland has three more years in office. Even if—if—he's impeached, which is impossible with Republicans controlling both sides of Congress, the worst he'll get is a slap on the wrist. He'll still be President."

Ethan had no argument for that. He knew she was right.

Natalie's voice softened. "Ethan... your graduate program ends in April. What happens to you then?"

Ethan hesitated before answering. "I'll be assigned to a foreign desk." He shrugged, as if it were a minor detail. "There's no indication I've been compromised. To everyone else, I'll just be some guy who studied abroad. I'll have a master's degree, and in time, I'll move up. One day, I'll be a handler, then a supervisor, then maybe—just maybe—a very senior CIA officer." He smirked, but it didn't reach his eyes. "I'll be fine, Natalie. I love my country. I'd die for it. And when Harland and his cronies are gone, my country will finally return to the values we claim to hold so dear."

A heavy silence settled between them. Natalie studied him, searching for something—hope, certainty, a promise that things would change.

April was just around the corner. Before she even had time to process it, Ethan Cole was gone.

23

POWER DWINDLING

The empire did not fall to an invading army, nor to the weight of external enemies pressing at its gates. It crumbled from within, the collapse inevitable, the rot festering at its very core long before the first cracks showed. Like a towering oak, proud and unyielding, the decay had begun deep in its trunk—where the eye could not see but where the structure was most vulnerable. The nucleus of power, once a source of strength, had become a wound, infected by arrogance, corruption, and unchecked ambition.

And when the fall came, it was swift—at least to those who had only ever seen the surface, who had mistaken outward grandeur for true stability. But in truth, the unraveling had begun long before. It had whispered in the corridors of power, in the secret betrayals and quiet shifts of loyalty, in the complacency of those who believed the status quo could never change. And so, in the end, it was not felled by an assassin's bullet or a foreign adversary, but by its own weight, collapsing into itself with a final, hollow creak.

So, it was with Harland.

The Triumvirate—a fragile, uneasy alliance—had rotted from the inside. Two men, each driven by ego and lust for power, had clashed. And one woman, charged with maintaining balance, had been forced to make a choice.

Margaret Kellerman chose survival.

She met with the Republican leadership in the Senate and the House. She laid it out clearly: President Harland was showing unmistakable signs of dementia. She had read enough about Reagan's final years in office to recognize the symptoms—the confusion, the reliance on scripted answers, the occasional lapses into incoherence. The President was slipping, and unlike Reagan, he had no Nancy to shield him.

The party elders listened. They were exhausted. The tariff war with Canada had bled their states dry, and the reckless push for annexation had only further alienated allies. They had no interest in welcoming forty million new Democratic voters into the union. Their loyalty to Harland had never been about him—it had been about power, and now, his presidency was becoming a liability.

Meanwhile, Winthrop was striking from the shadows. He wielded the vast media empire he had built, unleashing a relentless assault on Harland's character. Every buried scandal, every murky business dealing, every whispered accusation about his predatory past was dredged up and broadcast in a never-ending loop. Even Harland's most fervent supporters—those who had once clung to his every word—began to waver. They trusted Winthrop's networks. And Winthrop's writers, well-paid and merciless, made certain that trust was rewarded with damning revelations.

And so, the coup came, not with guns or tanks, but in a private meeting room in the White House.

The List

Harland, unaware of the ambush, entered expecting praise. Kellerman had told him the senior senators and representatives wanted to celebrate his achievements, to recognize his legacy. He had always loved the sound of applause, the affirmation of his own greatness. But there would be none of that today.

The Republican Senate Leader stood first. In his hands was a document—thick, weighty, final.

He began with the numbers. The President's approval rating had reached the lowest in American history. Then he passed the paper to Harland, who stared down at the signatures of every Red State governor. The message was clear: the tariffs had to go. The economies of their states—states that had once been the backbone of his support—were in ruins. The retaliatory tariffs from Canada, Mexico, and China had gutted their farmers. They needed their markets back. They needed stability.

Harland, momentarily stunned, recovered with bluster. He raged, calling them weak, spineless. He accused them of lacking "gumption." He pounded the table. But this time, he was shouted down.

For the first time in his political life, Harland found himself powerless.

Then, the Senate Leader placed another document in front of him.

It was a list. "These are the names of your new cabinet members," he said. "Effective immediately."

Harland stared at it, his face tightening. His entire cabinet—every department head, every senior advisor—was being removed. Secretary of State, Secretary of Defence, Attorney General, all gone. The replacements had already been selected, vetted, and, in some cases, sworn in behind his back. The message was clear: he was a figurehead now, a puppet in his own administration.

His stomach twisted. One name remained on the list—Margaret Kellerman.

The Senate Leader saw him notice and smirked. "She's been working with us to ensure a smooth transition. We've deemed her indispensable."

The words hit like a gut punch. Kellerman—his most trusted advisor—had been orchestrating this behind his back. She wasn't just a survivor. She was a player.

Harland's fists clenched. He was surrounded.

For a long moment, Harland said nothing. Then, with the weight of inevitability crushing down upon him, he nodded.

The Speech

That evening, the networks cut into their regular programming. Every major station carried the broadcast. Across the country, Americans sat in their living rooms, waiting.

The screen flickered, and there he was.

The President, his usual bravado hollowed out, sat at the Resolute Desk. His face was pale under the harsh studio lights. He gripped the edges of his speech as if it were the only thing keeping him steady.

"My fellow Americans," he began, his voice forced and brittle, "tonight, I come before you with an important announcement…"

The words were not his. They had been written for him. Every phrase carefully crafted; every inflection rehearsed. He spoke of unity, of economic strength, of the need for cooperation. He painted the surrender as a victory.

But as the speech went on, something in his expression changed. He knew.

He was no longer in control. By the time the cameras cut away, the American people had witnessed something they had never seen before: a president reduced to a figurehead. A leader, forced to yield.

Power, once absolute, had dwindled. And the empire, though it still stood, would never be the same again.

Prime Minister Lacroix's Address to the Nation

[Broadcast on Major Canadian Networks]

Fellow Canadians,

Tonight, I stand before you with a message of progress, partnership, and a reaffirmation of Canada's enduring role in the world. After months of determined negotiations, I am pleased to announce that the United States has lifted the tariffs that strained our economic relationship. In response, Canada will be removing all countermeasures—effective immediately.

This moment is not one for celebration at another's expense. We know that the United States remains a formidable power, ever conscious of its position on the global stage. We also know that our nation, rich in rare earth minerals and fresh water, holds resources our southern neighbor will inevitably seek. But Canada does not thrive by standing in defiance or by retreating in fear. We thrive by standing firm in our values, by working with our allies, and by recognizing that strength is not measured in size alone.

Prime Minister Pierre Elliott Trudeau once compared our relationship with the United States to that of a mouse sleeping beside an elephant. He said:

"Living next to you is in some ways like sleeping with an elephant. No matter how friendly and even-tempered the beast, one is affected by every twitch and grunt."

He was right then, and he remains right today.

We cannot ignore the weight of our neighbour's presence, nor should we. But we must also remember that history offers us another perspective—one of cooperation, of mutual reliance, and of the power of goodwill.

This is a victory not for one government, not for one leader, but for all Canadians who believe in the power of diplomacy, in economic cooperation, and in the value of treating our neighbours with both fairness and resolve.

We remain vigilant. We remain strong. But most of all, we remain Canadian—true to our values, true to our place in the world, and true to our belief that even the smallest among us can make a difference.

Thank you. Bonne soirée.

24

FAREWELL, LENNY

A Warrior's Final Battle

Lenny Bishop had fought many battles in his life—some as a young RCMP officer, others through the relentless pursuit of truth with True North, Strong and Free. But the greatest battle, the one he couldn't win, was the one raging inside him.

The cancer was a ruthless enemy, hollowing him out day by day. He no longer hid the weight loss beneath loose clothing, no longer made excuses for his fatigue. His world had shrunk to the walls of his apartment, where every movement was a test of will.

Natalie Cheng took leave from work to be with him. She sat by his side for hours, sometimes talking, sometimes just holding his hand in silence. Lenny's once-booming voice had softened into hoarse whispers, but his spirit never dulled. He still cracked a joke when he could, still muttered insults at the news when President Harland appeared on-screen, still clenched his fists at the thought of Canada brought to its knees by American greed.

Even as his body betrayed him, his mind refused to surrender. But surrender wasn't his choice to make.

A Friday Night with Friends

Word spread quickly that Lenny didn't have much time left.

On a cool Friday evening, the regulars from Hustlers—the pub where so many of his plans had been set in motion—brought the happy hour to him. They crowded into his apartment, bringing beer and laughter, telling old stories, war stories, bar fights, and moments of triumph. Lenny, propped up in his recliner, a glass of whiskey resting untouched on the table beside him, listened with tired but twinkling eyes.

"You stubborn old bastard," one of them said. "You never knew when to quit."

Lenny smirked. "Apparently, even now."

The laughter filled the room, drowning out the quiet ticking of time slipping away.

Family Comes Home

The following day, Randy arrived with his wife and four children—ages four to thirteen—the grandkids Lenny never spent enough time with. The apartment felt alive, filled with the energy of youth, with tiny hands reaching for him, hesitant smiles from children too young to understand why everyone spoke in soft voices.

Reggie came too. Clean-shaven. Sober. Working again. He had fought his own demons, and for once, it looked like he was winning.

Lenny didn't have the strength to say much, but the pride in his eyes spoke louder than words.

A Visit from the Past

Inspector Ron McDavid of the RCMP came that evening. He stood in the doorway for a moment, hesitant, then crossed the room with a firm handshake and a nod of respect.

"Lenny, you did good. With True North, Strong and Free. With your service. With everything."

Lenny's voice was weak but unwavering. "Did we stop him, McDavid?"

McDavid didn't hesitate. "Yes."

Lenny exhaled, the tension in his shoulders easing. He had given everything to stop Harland's aggression, to defend Canada's sovereignty against a man who had once thought the country was his for the taking.

Now, it was up to others to carry the fight forward.

The Final Hours

Lenny drifted in and out of consciousness over the next few days. His body was shutting down. He no longer ate, no longer spoke. He slept more than he was awake, his breaths shallow and uneven.

On the evening of June 5, 2026, with Natalie at his side, he opened his eyes one last time.

She squeezed his hand. "I'm here."

A flicker of a smile. A final breath.

And then he was gone.

A Life Worth Celebrating

A week later, the gathering room at Spears Funeral Home in downtown Regina was filled to capacity.

Family. Friends. Colleagues from True North, Strong and Free. Old RCMP comrades.

They had come not just to mourn, but to celebrate.

Natalie took the podium. She spoke not just as a friend and neighbor, but as someone who had fought beside him.

"Lenny Bishop was not a perfect man." A small chuckle rippled through the room. "He was stubborn. He was reckless. And he didn't always make the best choices. But he fought for something bigger than himself. He fought for this country. He fought for all of us."

She paused; voice thick with emotion.

"Canada is still standing today because of him."

A murmur of agreement swept through the crowd.

And then, from somewhere in the back, a voice called out—a familiar toast from Hustlers, one Lenny had raised many times before:

"To Lenny Bishop!"

The room echoed it. "To Lenny!"

Glasses lifted.

Tears fell.

And Lenny's fight, his legacy, would never be forgotten.

POST NOTE
WINTHROP'S FINAL BETRAYAL

Winthrop's Private Island – Undisclosed Location in the Caribbean

Grant Winthrop sat in the dimly lit conference room of his island compound, the warm ocean breeze barely reaching through the high-tech climate-controlled walls. His personal fortress was designed to function as both a corporate headquarters and an impenetrable safe haven.

Seated around him were three men, each representing a global superpower with a personal stake in America's decline:

- Viktor Orlov, a top Kremlin strategist with close ties to the Russian Ministry of Defence.

- Zhao Xun, an elite economic advisor to the Chinese Communist Party, known for spearheading Beijing's technological expansions.
- General Reza Barzani, Iran's chief military procurement officer, a man responsible for smuggling Western technology into Tehran's defence programs.

Each of them had flown in under the strictest secrecy, their private aircraft landing on a secluded airstrip built deep in the island's jungle. Winthrop had ensured every counter-surveillance measure was in place. No satellites, no leaks, no risk.

Because tonight, he wasn't just making a business deal. He was selling out the United States.

The Offer

Winthrop leaned back, exuding the same calculated ease that had made him one of the most dangerous men in Washington. He tapped a finger on his tablet, sending encrypted files onto the large screen behind him.

What appeared next stole the breath from his guests. The complete framework of the U.S. Federal Government's Payment System.

"This," Winthrop began, his voice smooth, "is what absolute access looks like."

On the screen, thousands of contracts flashed by—military procurement orders, classified research grants, CIA and NSA black budgets, even the disguised foreign aid agreements funnelled through intelligence cutouts.

"The American government trusted me with its deepest financial infrastructure," he continued. "Harland granted me full integration into their payment system. Every military contract, every intelligence operation, every covert arms deal—it all passes through my networks."

Zhao Xun folded his hands, his expression unreadable. "And you're willing to part with this?"

"For the right price," Winthrop confirmed.

Viktor Orlov let out a low chuckle, taking a sip of his vodka. "This is treason, Mr. Winthrop. Even for a man in exile."

Winthrop smirked. "Treason is just a matter of who writes the laws."

Barzani, the most impatient of the group, leaned forward. "What exactly are you offering?"

Winthrop swiped across his tablet again. The screen changed to a new dataset—his proprietary AI warfare programs.

"I'm not just giving you access," he said. "I'm giving you the future."

The files detailed next-generation artificial intelligence systems developed under Winthrop Technologies, many of them in joint projects with the Pentagon before Harland's collapse. These included:

- Autonomous combat drone networks capable of running independent operations with minimal human oversight.
- AI-powered cyber warfare units, able to breach Western financial systems, reroute transactions, and cripple economies without firing a single shot.
- Predictive war-gaming models, which had been tested by the U.S. Joint Chiefs of Staff, simulating full-scale global conflict scenarios.

Barzani's eyes flickered with interest. Iran's military was desperate to bridge the technological gap with Israel and the West. This was the edge they needed.

Orlov, however, was more interested in the financial chaos such data could cause. With this access, Russia could manipulate global oil markets, disrupt NATO defence spending, and redirect American military assets without them even knowing.

Zhao, ever the strategist, remained silent. China's ambitions were long-term. Control of this data meant the slow, methodical dismantling of U.S. global influence—without ever firing a missile.

The Price of Betrayal

Winthrop tapped his fingers against the table. "I assume you're all interested?"

The three men exchanged glances.

Zhao was the first to speak. "We need assurances."

Winthrop smirked. "Of course."

He swiped again, revealing the kill switch protocol he had embedded in his AI systems. Any attempt by the U.S. government to reclaim these networks would be met with total shutdown. Every system, every file, every AI model—all rigged for self-destruction the moment Washington tried to override his controls.

"America built itself on the illusion of unchallenged superiority," he said smoothly. "What I'm offering you is a way to prove that illusion is over."

The room was silent.

Then Orlov exhaled, a slow, knowing grin spreading across his face. "We'll pay. But I assume you have conditions?"

Winthrop nodded. "Two."

"One, this remains quiet. If this leaks too early, I lose leverage—and so do you."

The three men nodded. Discretion was understood.

"And two…" Winthrop's gaze darkened. "I want Harland to suffer."

The Final Blow

As the meeting concluded, Zhao Xun stood last, shaking Winthrop's hand with a firm grip. "Consider it done."

Within hours, encrypted financial transactions were processed through shadow banking networks in Hong Kong, Switzerland, and Dubai. Winthrop had just secured his next empire—outside of America's reach.

But the real destruction was still to come.

- Russia began quietly deploying cyber warfare teams to infiltrate the already-compromised U.S. Treasury system.
- China prepared a massive financial strike, leveraging AI algorithms to destabilize U.S. markets and weaken the dollar.
- Iran accelerated its military AI integration, moving years ahead of schedule in missile targeting and cyber warfare capabilities.

Back in Washington, Harland had no idea what was coming.

He thought he had ousted his rival.

But Grant Winthrop had already written America's obituary.

Final Scene: Harland's Panic

Oval Office – The Next Morning

President Jefferson Harland sat at his desk, his eyes glued to the emergency financial reports streaming in from the Federal Reserve and Treasury Department.

- Massive funds had been rerouted overnight.
- Several top military contracts were suddenly "lost" in bureaucratic limbo.
- The U.S. dollar was experiencing an "unexplained market fluctuation."

Margaret Kellerman burst into the room, holding a classified folder. "Mr. President," she said, her voice tight, "We have a problem."

Harland's hands trembled as he grabbed the file. The headline on the intelligence report read:

"GRANT WINTHROP RE-EMERGES: GLOBAL ESPIONAGE & FINANCIAL SABOTAGE LINKED TO EXILED U.S. TYCOON"

Harland's pulse pounded in his ears.

Winthrop. That son of a bitch had outplayed him.

And now? The entire world was about to burn.

ACKNOWLEDGMENTS

All my books have resulted from a considerable contribution from friends and family. My wife, Vivian, has dedicated her skills and time to all of my books since I started writing.

And of course, I thank Gina Jestadt, owner of Joose Publishing, for her continuing support and skills in publishing my books. If there are writers out there who do not know about self-publishing, I encourage them to reach out to Gina. You will not be sorry.

ABOUT THE AUTHOR

Keith Landry – Award-Winning Canadian Author & Master Storyteller

Keith Landry is a celebrated Canadian author whose riveting narratives breathe life into the untold stories of our nation's past. With a masterful blend of historical accuracy and compelling storytelling, Keith has captivated readers with 25 powerful stories, each inspired by real news articles that once graced the pages of Canadian history.

A late bloomer in the literary world, Keith began his writing journey at the age of 69, proving that passion knows no bounds. In just five years, he has established himself as a formidable force in historical fiction, earning accolades for his immersive storytelling. His book, *Unforeseen Saskatchewan*, was awarded the **International Impact Book Award** in the adventure category, solidifying his place among Canada's most compelling contemporary writers.

What makes Keith Landry's books unmissable?

- He masterfully transports readers to pivotal moments in Canadian history, weaving human emotion into real-life events.
- His work illuminates the triumphs and tragedies of everyday people, shedding light on stories that shaped our country.
- From gripping true crime to haunting disasters and love stories intertwined with history, his books offer a cinematic experience in literary form.

Keith's books have been praised for their meticulous research, depth of character, and ability to paint vivid portraits of the past. Readers describe his work as "impossible to put down," "a journey through time," and "deserving of a stage or screen adaptation."

Living in **Regina, Saskatchewan,** with his beloved wife **Vivian,** Keith continues to write stories that preserve history and spark conversation. Whether through **historical fiction, true crime, or adventure,** his books are a testament to the enduring power of storytelling.

For media inquiries, publishing opportunities, or to learn more about his work, reach out today!

📚 Contact Keith Landry

✉ Email: Kvlandry@hotmail.com

📞 Phone: 306-216-5318

📍 Address: 5005 Snowbirds Crescent, Regina, Saskatchewan, S4W 0H5

Hi Keith,

I started reading the manuscript and could not put it down. Even though you are preaching to the choir with me, I was in the edge of my seat with the Elon Musk character. There were twists and turns in the story than the road down to get into Sarajevo. This will get people thinking about their positions on many issues related to our current predicaments brought on by a clown who is turning the world into a circus. No doubt there will be many armchair analysts judging every politician's decisions. And many of those opinions coloured by their partisan biases. The thing that draws it all together is the inclusion of the big world actors that are sitting on the periphery ready to clean up after the mess. None of us will be unaffected by the consequences of what is transpiring today.

I would gladly accept the books and give them to people who love talking about these issues.

- Murray

ALSO BY KEITH LANDRY

The Garden Detectives

Allumette Island Massacre

Silent Nights, Deadly Days in the Pontiac

The Boarding School at the End of the Dirt Road

Broken Bottle

Black Tuesday A Canadian Love Story

Frontier Resilience

All Roads Lead to Campbell's Bay

Murders Tales from the Archives

Murder Tales from the Ottawa Valley

Murder Tales from the Ottawa Valley, Volume 2

Canadian Catastrophes

Blood in the Headlines

Shadows of Melfort

Motley Crooks

Unforeseen Saskatchewan

The Dalpe Collection

Dalpe's Chronicles

Dalpe and the Nazi

Dalpe and the Communist Spies

Dalpe and the Missing Men

Dalpe and the Roots of Evil

The Hermit Murder

The Jungle Murder

Maniwaki Mystery Death

Dalpe's Crime Chronicles

2024 INTERNATIONAL IMPACT BOOK AWARDS

- WINNER -

AWARDED TO

Keith Landry

Unforeseen Saskatchewan

Adventure - Action Adventure

Presented by International Impact Book Awards
December, 2024

Manufactured by Amazon.ca
Acheson, AB